P9-ARA-648

THE MEMORY OF LOVE

Also by Jim Fergus

Fiction

One Thousand White Women: The Journals of May Dodd

The Wild Girl: The Notebooks of Ned Giles

Marie-Blanche

Nonfiction

A Hunter's Road

The Sporting Road

Jim Fergus

THE MEMORY OF LOVE

Cover photograph: Chrysis Jungbluth on the docks at Cherbourg, France, 1929.
Private collection of Clément Relouzat

The Memory of Love was published in France with the original title *Chrysis* © Jim Fergus, *2013*.
French translation © le cherche midi, 2013.
23, rue du Cherche-Midi 75006 Paris
www.cherche-midi.com

For information address Jim Fergus LLC, P.O. Box 8099, Tumacacori, AZ 85640.
www.jimfergus.com

ISBN: 1490904867
ISBN 13: 9781490904863

To Isabella

"It is because sensuality is a condition, mysterious but necessary and creative, of intellectual development. Those who have not felt to their limit the strongest demands of the flesh, whether as a blessing or as a curse, are incapable of understanding fully the demands of the spirit. Just as the beauty of the soul illumines the features, so only the virility of the body nourishes the brain. The worst insult that Delacroix could address to men—that he hurled indiscriminately at those who railed against Rubens and Ingres—was this terrible word: "Eunuchs!"

Better yet, it seems that the genius of races, like that of individuals, is, before all, sensual. All the cities which have reigned over the world—Babylon, Alexandria, Athens, Rome, Venice, Paris—have been by a general law, all the more licentious as they were powerful, as though their dissoluteness were necessary to their splendor."

Pierre Louÿs, *Aphrodite: Ancient Manners*

Foreword

In the summer of 2007, a year before the death of my partner, Mari Tudisco, I took her to a renowned cancer clinic in Bavaria, Germany for a consultation. It was one of those exclusive, hushed, vine-covered private institutions to which celebrities and the wealthy slip discreetly away to seek miracle cures reputedly unavailable elsewhere. In this way, before it was all over and Mari breathed her last brave, rattled breath in the hospice facility the following summer, she would try everything from clinical trial chemotherapy treatments, to holistic cures, to the ministrations of a Huichol Indian shaman said to own the gift of healing.

This summer of 2007 would be our last good summer, our last trip together to Europe. Mari was still relatively strong, and even though she knew in her heart that she was dying, she maintained her tremendous sense of *joie de vivre*; she laughed and loved and lived her life as she always had, as if each day might be her last. "We must accept finite disappointment," said Martin Luther King, "but never lose infinite hope."

The consultation at the Bavarian clinic offered little in the way of hope; the doctor there told us that Mari should continue following the course of treatment prescribed by her physicians in America, that they were doing everything possible given the advanced nature of her cancer. And so we returned to Nice, where we had left Mari's 16-year-old daughter, Isabella, in a tennis camp.

On our first day back, Mari and I were wandering around the Old Port of the city, browsing in antique stores and galleries, which had always been one of our favorite activities together. Indeed, we had first met, six years earlier, in such a place in Tucson, Arizona. Now we walked into one of the antique shops; it was cluttered, disorganized, and dusty, the common natural state of these establishments. I can smell now the musty scent of that store, can see still the slightly dim interior, the jumble of old objects waiting for new life, the dust hanging languidly in the thin beams of sunlight that entered through the crusty windows, all so vivid in my memory of that day. It is both the joy and the pain of this writing life, the conjuring up of our ghosts to the page where they live on forever.

And now Mari stops before a painting resting on the floor, propped against the legs of an old rusted iron garden chair. It is unframed, frayed around the edges, damaged in spots.

"Jim, come look at this," she says. And as I approach she picks the painting up, sets it on the seat of the chair, and takes a step back to study it. Mari is herself a gifted painter, with a fine eye for art. "I love this. Don't you love it?"

"Yes, I do."

"I think the artist was quite young when she painted it," she says.

"How would you know that?"

"Because there is such a sense of joy and innocence about it. It is so full of the spirit and wonder of youth. Don't you see it?"

"I see a bunch of naked people having a lot of fun!" I say, laughing.

"Yes, exactly!'

I look on the back of the canvas; a tag is pinned to the stretcher bar, noting the price, and: *"Orgie", Chrysis Jungbluth, v. 1925.* And beneath that:

JUNGBLUTH, Chrysis. Boulogne-sur-mer, 23 janvier 1907 -

"Well, if it is accurately dated, you're right about one thing. She was roughly 18-years-old when she painted this."

"Can we buy it?" Mari asks.

In America, one quickly discovers over the course of a long terminal illness the utter inadequacy of one's health insurance, how expensive a slow death truly is.

"I'm sorry, sweetheart, I just can't do it right now."

Mari smiles gently, "Of course, I understand."

We returned to the United States, and Mari resumed her cancer treatments, and the long agonizing journey we must all make to ash, to dust. Some weeks later, I came upon the business card I had taken from the antique store in Nice, and I remembered again the painting and Mari's pleasure in it. It is remarkable the things we do, the totems we collect, as if secretly hoping that they might possess some magic properties to keep our doomed loved ones alive. And so on a kind of impulse, I phoned the proprietor and I asked him if he still had *Orgie*. Yes, he said, he did. I purchased it via a bank transfer, and he shipped it to me in America, where I had it professionally restored and framed.

One evening during the Christmas holidays, when Isabella was spending the night at a cousin's house, I gave the painting to Mari as my last Christmas gift to her. She was quite ill by now, very frail and thin, but she had always possessed a childlike side; indeed, all her life Mari exuded that same spirit of joy, innocence and wonder she had identified upon first viewing *Orgie.* And now when I unveiled it before her, her face brightened, her eyes flashed and as sick as she was she became in that instant a young woman again, filled with all the hope and promise of life. "You bought it after all!" she said.

Mari studied the painting for a long time. "I want you to keep this for now," she said, finally. "And after I'm gone, I want Isabella to have it."

"Well, of course, it's yours and then it will be hers," I answered. "But just out of curiosity, why does a mother want her 16-year-old daughter to have a painting depicting an orgy?"

"I'll tell you why," Mari said. "You know as well as anyone that I've always been kind of ashamed of my body, embarrassed to show it; I've always had a complex about exposing myself. I don't want Bella to be that way. I want her to feel as free about her body as these women. Look how happy they are, and so completely without shame. I love that! That's what I want for my daughter, I want her to feel the same sense of freedom, to feel good in her own skin."

Mari died seven months later, and three weeks after that Isabella began her senior year of high school. Bella's biological father had died when she was nine-years-old, and Mari had appointed me to be her legal guardian. And so I looked after her that year, before sending her off to college the following fall.

I did not show Bella the painting until Christmas of 2009, a year and half after her mother's death, and exactly two years after I had first given it to Mari. Bella was 18-years-old then, becoming overnight a young woman, filled with her own dreams and hopes. She loved *Orgie* on first sight, in the same way her mother had that day in Nice. I explained that it belonged to her now, but that I would keep it until she had finished her education and had a place of her own.

"I just want to be clear about one thing, Bella," I said. "Your mom did not want you to have this painting in order to encourage you to participate in orgies!" And I told her what Mari had said to me.

After she returned to her college in Vermont at the end of the holidays, Isabella phoned me one afternoon. She had been chosen to write an essay on a subject of her choice, and to read it in front of the entire university—the student body, the faculty and deans. She had decided that she was going to write about *Orgie*, and why her mother wished for her to have it, and she asked me questions about the artist, and the date of the painting. I was busy finishing a long overdue novel whose progress had been delayed by Mari's illness and death, and by my own grief process, all of which had largely closed me down creatively for several years. I knew little more about Chrysis Jungbluth then than I had when Mari and I first saw *Orgie* in the antique store in Nice. By now I had found photographs of some of her other work online, but I still knew nothing more about her personal life than this:

JUNGBLUTH, Chrysis. Boulogne-sur-mer, January 23, 1907 -

Isabella wrote a lovely essay about her mother and the painting. She is a fine writer, a gifted poet, a smart, kind, thoughtful young lady. But she had always been a rather timid child. Indeed, in this regard, Bella was quite unlike her mother, who all her life was ready for any new experience, every adventure. Mari had always pushed her daughter to try new things—to hike mountains, to swim in the sea, to eat unfamiliar dishes—and not always successfully.

Isabella performed her essay in the college auditorium, and afterwards she phoned me to tell me about it.

"So how did it go, Bella?" I asked.

"Pretty well, I think."

"Your essay was well-received?"

"Yeah, I think so," she said. "When I finished the reading, I opened my shirt."

"You did what?"

"I opened my shirt. You know at the end of the essay, after I told why my mom wanted me to have the painting, I unbuttoned my shirt and opened it."

"You exposed yourself in front of the whole college?"

"Yeah."

"And, of course, you weren't wearing a bra, right?"

"That was sort of the whole point, wasn't it?" she asked.

There was a long pause on the line, as I thought this over. "Wow, Bella…" I said finally, "your mom would be so proud of you."

Such was the genesis of my search for the young artist named Chrysis Jungbluth—the discovery of this painting on the floor of the antique store in the *Vieux Port* of Nice. And if the painting itself was the seed of this novel, Isabella exposing her breasts to her university was its first sprout. Bella was roughly the same age as Chrysis Jungbluth had been when she painted *Orgie,* and now across the decades and through the medium of art, Mari had introduced these young women to each other. And somehow, I felt responsible for both of them.

I finished my long overdue family novel at last, a full seven years after I had started it. The painting, *Orgie,* now hung in my living room and I looked at it everyday, and everyday I tried to imagine the life of the artist. I began doing some research of my own, searching for Chrysis's trail, at the very least hoping to put a date at the end of that inconclusive dash. I traveled to France, and spent some days at the Bibliothèque des Beaux-Arts, the Bibliothèque Nationale, and the Bibliothèque de l'INHA; I spoke to gallery owners and art historians, and on a wet, gloomy winter day I took the train up to Boulogne-sur-Mer, to see the town where the infant Chrysis had been born. Very gradually, the path of her life began to unfold before me. I followed it, and I am still following it.

Although the real names of a number of actual historical figures are used in this book, including, of course, the young artist Chrysis Jungbluth, this is a novel, a fiction, an act of imagination, and the characters here portrayed are strictly fictional re-creations.

Jim Fergus
Rand, Colorado
November 1, 2012

THE MEMORY OF LOVE

BOGEY

1916

1

In the spring of 1916, 17-year-old Bogart "Bogey" Lambert rode out from his family's ranch in North Park, Colorado on a dappled gray stallion named Crazy Horse, headed to France to join the Foreign Legion and fight against the Huns in the Great War.

Bogey's father had refused to say goodbye to his only son, leaving the house early that morning on the pretext of checking an irrigation head gate in the upper hay meadow. But now his mother ran after him, calling, carrying an extra sandwich and a piece of rhubarb pie wrapped in waxed paper, inside a paper bag. Bogey reined up Crazy Horse.

"Your father doesn't understand why you're leaving us," his mother said as she caught up to him. She spoke this as a simple statement of fact, rather than one of accusation or blame; she knew better than to try to stop her son now. Bogey had always had a mind of his own, ever since he was a young boy, a romantic, independent streak, and a stubbornness. Once he set his mind to something, there was no turning him back. "He just doesn't understand why you're so determined to go off to fight for a country that isn't even yours."

"We got French blood, Mama," Bogey said. "You told me so yourself. You told me my name came from France. Bogart, 'the strength of the bow,' you always said it meant."

"Our French blood is three generations old, Bogey," she said. "We don't even have the language anymore."

"I'll learn the language."

"Do you even know how to get there, son?" she asked. "You do know that you can't ride Crazy Horse all the way to France, don't you?"

"Mama, I took geography," Bogey said. "I'll make inquiries in Denver about the trains east. And when I get there, I'll hire onto a ship to cross the sea. I'll find my way."

"I expect you will, Bogey," she said. "But what will you do with Crazy Horse?"

"I'm going to take him down to the sale barn in Fort Collins," Bogey said. "I'll need the extra cash for my grubstake."

"There is something else inside this bag with your sandwich and pie that might help you a bit in that way, son," his mother said.

"Don't worry about me, Mama, please. I can take care of myself."

She nodded sadly. She knew that he could. "Goodbye then, my boy, you be sure to write us now."

"Of course I will," Bogey said. "Goodbye, Mama." He reined his horse around, lightly touching its flanks with his heels until Crazy Horse broke into an easy lope. Bogey did not dare look back at his mother, or at the ranch, for he was crying now at leaving the only world he had ever known.

2

For two years Bogey Lambert had been reading articles in the *Rocky Mountain News* about the war in Europe. He bought penny periodicals at the general store in town; they were filled with lurid drawings of giant leering German soldiers plunging bayonets into the smaller, prostrate French troops, the battlefield littered with bloody corpses. Bogey was at that age when the notion of war still seemed impossibly romantic, and somehow abstract; he imagined himself as a character in one of those drawings, riding heroically into the scene, wielding at once both lance and six-shooter, cutting down the evil Huns left and right, single-handedly saving France, land of his ancestors, from the ravages of the aggressors.

Bogey had a talent for writing, and he wrote stories in his notebook about his imagined exploits, though he knew virtually nothing about France other than what he read in the newspaper and the periodicals, and in outdated history books available in the small town library. His stories were largely fanciful juvenilia, and when he would look back at them many years later, after having actually witnessed the unspeakable carnage of the Great War, he would wonder why his parents hadn't simply locked him in the root cellar until his adolescence had passed.

Bogey was a tall, lean, long-limbed boy, with ropy, supple muscles, strong for his age, a gifted calf roper, bronc rider, and fast draw trick shooter. In the summertime he competed in regional rodeos and county fairs in Colorado, Nebraska, Wyoming and Montana, against cowboys almost always older than he. He was a fine natural athlete and a consummate horseman, and he won events often enough that he managed to save a little nest egg of prize money. This he supplemented by working odd jobs off the ranch when his father didn't need him, and he saved that money, too.

As a young man, Bogey's father had spent a few years pursuing a boxing career in Denver, and he began coaching his son in the sport at a young age. Sometimes traveling circuses came through town, with a professional prizefighter as one of their acts. A ring was set up, and the fighter would take on all comers from the audience, with much wagering between the circus hawker and the locals—another way to fleece the country bumpkins. These prizefighters were usually well past their prime, large, heavyset men, scarred and hardened from too many years at their profession. They generally lacked finesse, relying on sheer strength and heavy punching to knock out their amateur opponents as quickly as possible. They knew all the dirty tricks of the game—the low blows and rabbit punches to the kidneys, the biting, the boxing gloves loaded with lead—and, to be sure, the circus referee never called fouls on them.

Bogey's father would sit beside him in the audience and they would watch a couple of other local men fight the professional first, and they would critique the circus boxer's performance, identifying his strengths and weaknesses. Then Bogey would raise his hand, and climb into the ring himself. The knowing townspeople, the local ranch families and cowboys would cheer, and with winks and secret smiles, would lay their bets with the circus hawker.

The professional pugilist sneered at Bogey's youth, his lean physique and boyishly smooth, unblemished face. He had, over the course of his long career, seen plenty of these cocky young cowboys climb into the ring to face him, and he seemed almost to take pity upon this one, moving in on the bell of the first round, smiling, intending to make short work of the fight without doing too much damage to his callow young opponent. He knew that he might well make the boy burst into tears after only one punch, which often happened with inexperienced young men who thought they were tough enough to take on an old veteran.

But now as the circus boxer stalked him, Bogey began to circle the man with the fluid dancing footwork his father had taught him, staying just out of his reach. Frustrated by the fact that he was unable to land a punch against this moving target, the professional finally swung wildly, which gave Bogey the opening he needed to move in himself and pummel the big man with a series of deadly fast combinations, before dancing back again. The crowd cheered, and the circus boxer's smile turned to a look of confusion and anger that he had underestimated this upstart. He bore down, no more pity for the youngster, his fists high, moving in on Bogey with his determined stalking gait, but still throwing punches he could not land, as the boy stayed just out of his reach. When the right moment came, the fighter tiring and off balance, Bogey stepped in, stunning him with a sharp left jab to the temple and then landing the "money punch," a brutally efficient right uppercut, and down the professional went. The partisan crowd erupted in wild cheering for their hometown prodigy. Indeed, precocious young Bogey Lambert, who had begun taking on these circus pros at the age of 15, was to date undefeated, and the grateful locals always shared a generous cut of their winnings with him.

Similarly, Bogey's father had trained him in the sport of fast draw shooting, and had presented his son when he was only nine-years-old with a Colt .45 Peacemaker revolver that had belonged to Bogey's grandfather, the former sheriff of Medicine Bow, Wyoming Territory, who was killed in 1876 in a showdown on Main Street, by an outlaw named Crazy Bill Bugler, who once rode with Jesse James.

"You know what the second place prize in a gunfight is, son?" his father had asked Bogey.

"No, sir," Bogey answered, "I did not know there was such a prize."

"That is correct, son," his father said, "because he who comes in second is dead. Now you get fast enough on the draw and you'll never have to worry about dying the way your grandpa did."

Fast draw shooting was an art that had fallen into some state of disuse since the wild west was won, but there were still exhibitions and competitions held at county fairs and rodeos in the region. Of course, rather than shooting at each other, competitors fired at targets, with stop-watches and accuracy determining the winner. Although at first Bogey could barely lift the Peacemaker, as in most things he undertook, he had a natural aptitude. As he grew and his arm strengthened, and after endless hours practicing in front of the mirror, he began to win a little prize money in that sport, as well. And so it was that Bogey had saved up enough of a nest egg, he believed, along with the future sale of his beloved mount, Crazy Horse, to take him all the way to France.

After a few hours ride, Bogey stopped on the banks of a creek, still swollen and muddy with spring runoff, and he pulled his mother's parting gift from his saddlebag. In addition to his sandwich and a piece of rhubarb pie, there was a small leather pouch inside, and when he opened it he found a thick wad of mostly small bills. When he counted them out the total came to $87, which seemed to Bogey a grand fortune. His mother was the teacher in the local one-room schoolhouse, and he knew that this was money she had put aside over the years from her small salary, for "a rainy day." The notion that she had given him her life savings so that he might pursue his own crazy dreams, of which she clearly did not approve, made Bogey start crying all over again. He wondered if maybe he should just turn around and ride back to the ranch; his parents would be so happy to see him, so grateful that he had come home.

He ate his sandwich and the piece of pie on the bank of the creek. Crazy Horse grazed nearby on the new shoots of tender, pale green grass. When Bogey had finished eating, he remounted, and then he just sat his horse for a time. He had been so sure of himself this morning when he rode out. But now he was scared and he just wanted to go home. He realized then that he was not nearly so tough as he thought, and he knew that whatever decision he made in this moment, one way or another, would inalterably change the course of his life, and after this there would be no turning back. And so he just sat there on Crazy Horse for a long time, thinking things over.

Finally he nodded to himself, and turned the collar of his canvas long rider coat up around his neck; it was still cool this time of year in the high country. He reined Crazy Horse south again toward Cameron Pass which ran between the Medicine Bows and the Never Summer Range, and which would take him down into Fort Collins. The snow wasn't yet off the high peaks of the mountains, but the lower slopes were already greening up. He knew that it would be a long time before he saw this country again, and he tried to absorb the full grandeur of the landscape, to imprint it in his mind and to carry it with him wherever he went and through whatever was to come.

Bogey rode on toward the pass. He would not cry again.

3

Bogey went down to the sale barn in Fort Collins to register Crazy Horse for the auction block. He filled out the papers and signed them, and the barn manager told him that his horse would be stabled there for a week, giving prospective buyers time to inspect him. Bogey took a room in a boarding house nearby, and he went down to the stable every day to visit Crazy Horse, and to feed him apples or carrots. "It's OK, old boy," he would whisper to his horse, "you'll have a good life on a nice ranch somewhere, doing what you like to do best—working cattle, breeding mares...it'll be just fine, you'll see," Bogey said, speaking as much to convince himself as he was to his horse.

On the morning of the auction in which Crazy Horse was listed, Bogey went early to the sale ring to sit in the stands. His would be the fifth horse on the block and when one of the handlers led him into the ring, Crazy Horse sidestepped nervously, wild-eyed and throwing his head. "Go gentle with that horse!" Bogey called out from the stands, "He won't fight you if you give him his head." But the handler paid no heed, and only tightened his grip on the lead rope.

Bogey got to his feet then, descended the bleachers, and bounded over the fence. "I said to go gentle with that horse," he repeated, approaching the handler, Crazy Horse's eyes calming when he saw his master. "Can't you see you're making him nervous?"

"Son, you ain't allowed here," said the auctioneer. "You need to clear out of the ring right now."

"I've changed my mind," Bogey said, "This horse is not for sale anymore."

"Way too late for that, son," said the auctioneer. "You ain't the first owner to have seller's remorse, believe me, but you already signed the papers."

"Give me that lead rope," Bogey said to the handler.

"I can't do that, kid."

"Sure you can, mister," Bogey said.

"Get this boy outta here," the auctioneer called to three other cowboys who were sitting languidly on the fence, smoking and watching the scene with amusement. But before the men could even climb off their fence rail, Bogey punched the handler in the face, and as the man went down, he took the lead rope from his hand. "Real sorry about that, mister," said Bogey, who was a polite boy, though the handler was already unconscious before he hit the dirt.

Now Bogey swung onto Crazy Horse's back as he had done thousands of times before, and guiding him with only the lead rope attached to the halter, he rode toward the far fence of the sale ring, Crazy Horse clearing it in an impressive leap that elicited a collective gasp from those in the stands, and caused one old rancher to remark, "I sure would like to have bid on *that* horse."

Bogey galloped from the premises, not stopping until they reached the boarding house, where he saddled Crazy Horse; fortunately he had not yet been able to bring himself to sell his tack. He strapped on his saddlebags and bedroll. Having come to the sudden, instinctive realization that his horse was all he had left of his old life on the family ranch, and that he was finally incapable of giving him up, Bogey made another snap decision: instead of taking the train, he was going to ride Crazy Horse across the country, all the way to New York City.

4

It was a journey of over two thousand miles, that would take Bogey and Crazy Horse eighty-three days and require ten sets of horseshoes. On the first leg of the long ride, it gave Bogey some solace to follow the Platte River from eastern Colorado through Nebraska, for its headwaters were in the mountains of his home country, and he imagined as he rode that he was a natural component of the water flowing beside him, both issuing from the same source, both traveling in the same direction, toward the sea.

Bogey had never before been outside of the western United States, and as he rode east the mountains faded farther away in the distance, until finally, when he turned around in the saddle to catch one last sight of them, they were gone altogether. It was a long, solitary journey through the American heartland, from Nebraska, southern Iowa, and central Illinois, through Indiana, Ohio, West Virginia, Pennsylvania. Bogey avoided cities and either camped out on the trail, or accepted the hospitality of kindly country folks along the way, who would sometimes offer him a hot meal and a bed for the night, or at least a place to sleep in their barn.

When finally they reached New York state in late August, Bogey made inquiries outside the city and found a man with a truck and a horse trailer who agreed to take him to the port in return for gas money. There he planned to find passage across the ocean on a freighter.

Having never before seen the sea, Bogey found it to be even bigger than he had imagined, and the immensity of the city itself intimidated him. But he was by nature a taciturn boy, who had learned to keep his own counsel, to be always vigilant and patient, as his father had taught him in his boxing training. And so it was that he closed up into himself as if in a kind of defensive boxing posture, his fists held high to protect his head, able to look out at this strange, busy, filthy city from within his own safe haven, and with a certain calmness and objectivity.

Bogey rented a stall for Crazy Horse at a stable in the harbor, and he took a room at a nearby boarding house, which was next door to a brothel that serviced the sailors who came to port. He went everyday to the Harbor Master's office to look at the list of incoming and outgoing ships posted on the bulletin board, and to inquire about those sailing to France. He hoped to secure passage soon, as the expense of lodging himself and Crazy Horse would mount quickly. But the routes and schedules of the French shipping lines had been greatly disrupted by the predations of German U-boats prowling the Atlantic, and by the fact that many of the cargo and passenger ships had been requisitioned by the French government for the war effort. Thus arrivals and departures were irregular and unreliable, and some ships that left port on one side of the ocean, never came in on the other.

Bogey's room at the boarding house was noisy at night due to the late activities at "Mona's" whorehouse next door. It was a raucous establishment, frequented by randy sailors who had been weeks or months at sea without the company of women. Lively music issued from the place at all hours, and there was much drinking and dancing and singing, laughing and hollering and fighting.

In the summer of Bogey's 15th year, while he had been competing in a rodeo in Cheyenne, some of his older friends had taken him to such an establishment. Substitute cowboys for sailors, and the plains of Wyoming for the sea of New York, and it was just like this. Bogey had been a virgin at the time, and his cowboy friends knew this and teased him relentlessly about it. But the girls at the cathouse liked him because he treated them with respect, even reverence, and in addition he was a handsome boy, gentle and loving and curious as he explored their bodies, discovering in the process his own, and the immense pleasures of the erotic life.

Every morning, after he had checked the list for incoming ships at the Harbor Master's office, Bogey went over to the stables and took Crazy Horse out for a ride around the harbor or into the countryside. He would often ride by the boarding house on these outings. Mona's would be quiet then at last, most of the girls still sleeping. The clatter of horseshoes on cobblestone would wake some of them, and when they looked out their windows, the handsome young cowboy riding straight in the saddle made rather a favorable impression upon them, as they did upon Bogey.

One morning a young woman came out the backdoor of Mona's and waved to him as he rode by. She was a pretty, sandy-haired girl with a slight figure, and Bogey took her to be roughly his age. He reined up and tipped his hat. "Afternoon, ma'am."

The girl smiled at his cowboy manners. "My mother wants to know if you'll come in and have a bite to eat and a cup of coffee with us?" she asked.

"Why, I'd be much obliged, ma'am," Bogey answered. "Who is your mother?"

"Mona, the owner," said the girl. "And I'm Lola. What's your name, cowboy?"

"Bogart Lambert, but most folks call me Bogey."

She smiled. "Bogey it is then," she said. "Around here, we just go by first names."

Bogey nodded. He remembered from his brief experience in Cheyenne that there was a certain etiquette to be observed at the whorehouse. He dismounted, tethered Crazy Horse and followed the girl inside the backdoor. Five other girls, in various states of undress, and with the sleep not quite yet out of their faces, sat around a large kitchen table, drinking coffee. A robust, broad-hipped woman, Mona herself, stood at the stove cooking bacon and eggs. She turned and wiped her hand on her apron when Bogey and the girl entered. He removed his cowboy hat.

"Can I offer you breakfast, young man?" she asked.

"I ate my breakfast some hours ago, ma'am," Bogey answered. "But I'd be pleased to have a bite of whatever you're offering if I may call it my supper." In his months on the road, Bogey had learned never to turn down a free meal.

Mona laughed. "You may call it whatever you wish, son," she said, turning back to the stove. "Sit down, make yourself at home. Lola, get the young man a cup of coffee."

The girls made a seat for him at the table and Bogey sat down among them. He smiled and ran the table with his eyes, feeling the inevitable twinge of teenage arousal. All these girls, he thought to himself with wonder, and all of them looking at him speculatively, with mildly amused looks on their faces.

"I'm Honey," said one.

"I'm Clara," said another.

"Ginger."

"Violet."

"Nellie."

"His name is Bogey, girls," said Lola, with a small, teasing laugh. "You know, like the 'bogeyman.'"

"Or you can call me Bogart," he said. "That's my real name. Real pleased to meet you ladies."

"That is a very interesting name, young Bogart," said Mona.

"It's old French, ma'am," said Bogey proudly. "A family name."

"We get a goodly number of French customers in here when their boats are in harbor," said Mona. "Always did like French men myself. They're more romantic than the Germans, Swedes or Americans, and they treat the girls better than the Italians and Spaniards. In this business, you come to appreciate a gentleman, Bogart. And by the way, please call me Mona."

"Yes, ma'am," he said. "I mean, yes, Mona."

"I have been watching you since you came to the neighborhood," she said, as she plated food for the table. I can see from the manner in which you comport yourself that you are a young man of strong character, and a gentleman. I suspect you are waiting for a ship, but in the meantime, I would like to offer you employment if you are so inclined."

"Indeed, I am so inclined, Mona," said Bogey. "I could sure use the income. And what sort of employment do you have available, if I may ask, ma'am?"

"We recently lost our house bouncer," said Mona. "Big Romanian fellow, perhaps you saw him around the neighborhood, went by the name of Vlad. He quit us without notice and hired onto a ship bound to Brazil. Being a close neighbor, you have surely noticed that things can get a bit rowdy in here from time to time. It is necessary to have a capable man on the premises to enforce the rules."

"And what are those, Mona?" Bogey asked.

"No fighting, no dirty language, no vomiting, and above all, no harming the girls," said Mona. "We run a clean operation here. Now it is true that you do not have quite the physical presence of Vlad, nor as intimidating a name. However, you do have the cowboy persona in your favor, and you are a big lad who looks like he can take care of himself in a tough spot. Does that sound like a position which you might be able to fill, young Bogart?"

"Why yes, ma'am, I believe I could. I have boxing experience, and I have a six-shooter with which I am pretty handy, if I may say so myself."

"The boxing is a useful attribute to bring to the job," said Mona, who was now passing out full plates to the table, "but we do try not to resort to firearms. Vlad's primary approach to unruly customers was to bite off a portion of an ear, which was an effective determent to bad behavior, albeit a messy one.

"As to your salary, it has three separate components if this suits you. Firstly, I provide free meals and lodging, which means that you can move out of the boarding house and into your own room here whenever you wish. Secondly, there is a weekly cash salary paid on Sundays, the details of which we will discuss in the privacy of my office. And thirdly," Mona said, sweeping her hand around the table, "if you so choose, and at your pleasure, you may avail yourself of the services of my fine staff here—outside of regular business hours, of course, and with their willing participation."

At this, Bogey blushed deeply, and the girls all giggled at his embarrassment.

"Does that sound like a satisfactory arrangement to you, Bogart?" Mona asked.

"Why yes…yes, ma'am…yes, Mona, it surely does," Bogey stammered, which elicited renewed giggles. "That sounds most satisfactory to me."

5

The days and the weeks passed, and still no suitable ship came into port from France. The hot city summer faded to a cool fall, mid-October now, the leaves on the eastern trees in full color.

Bogey had settled comfortably at Mona's, and other than the late hours, and having to deal with drunken, quarrelsome sailors on a nightly basis, he was quite happy there. It was not difficult work; he broke up fights periodically, and sometimes had to fight himself, but with his boxing skills and the fact that his opponents were almost always drunk when they got out of line, these fights were usually short-lived and one-sided. And in the rare event that Bogey's fists were not sufficient to subdue a particularly truculent sailor, Mona had supplied him with a policeman's walnut billy club, which made short work of even the most troublesome customer.

So it was that the "cowboy bouncer" as Bogey became known in the harbor, began to achieve a reputation as one not to be trifled with, resulting in a gradual improvement in the general comportment of the clientele. Bogey was protective of his girls, and by far the harshest physical punishment he meted out was to those who mistreated them in any way. Well brought up by his mother, he believed in the sanctity of womanhood. For their part, the girls grew fond of the young cowboy, so different than their usual customers, and they were eager to express their gratitude.

And so Bogey took full advantage of the services of Mona's staff—his supplementary salary—immersing himself in a thoroughly hedonistic sensual life, which, moreover, was great fun and full of laughter.

It was, all considered, a dream job for a young man. Growing up on the ranch, Bogey had, for his entire life, risen at dawn or earlier. But now due to the long nights that stretched into morning, he often didn't wake until midday, and then sometimes in a tangle of bodies with two or three of the girls in his bed, all of them curled together like a litter of sleeping puppies. Perhaps he would make love then with one or two of them who were awake, the slow, gentle coupling of morning, the girls' skin warm and musty with sleep. And then perhaps they would all doze off again.

In this way, Bogey became a friend as well as a lover to the girls, a kind of confidante with whom they shared their dreams for a future that did not involve offering sexual services to drunken sailors. He listened to their stories, and he wrote them down in his notebook. They were just young woman with the same hopes and aspirations as any others, though they almost always came from hard backgrounds—poverty, broken families, alcoholic parents, abusive fathers—all things about which Bogey knew absolutely nothing from his own life experience. Some wanted family—husbands, children, security—others dreamed simply of a life of travel and adventure, although how they might go about this in reality remained a vaguely inchoate notion. Now and then a girl actually did leave Mona's, to take another job in the city, or on a ship, and occasionally one would run off with an impulsive young sailor who had fallen in love with her. Often these girls were never heard from again, but sometimes they came back, meek and defeated, to resume their former profession.

Bogey developed a special relationship with young Lola, whose mother, Mona, was grooming her to take over the family business. As Lola was "management" and did not work as one of the "girls," Mona had made it quite clear to Bogey from the beginning that her daughter was not included in the offer of his supplementary salary. In her case, the policy for him to follow was strictly hands-off. Nevertheless, Mona had grown fond of Bogey, and when she saw a certain romance blossoming between the two of them, she did not discourage it. Out of respect for his employer, Bogey maintained a chaste relationship with Lola, although, of course, the girl knew about his sexual adventures with the staff.

On Sundays, the one day of the week when Mona's was closed, Bogey would rent a second horse at the stables and he and Lola would go out riding together. Often they took picnics along with them. There was still pristine countryside just outside the loud, dirty crush of the port, and on his day off, Bogey always felt the need for some infusion of nature into his life, some space, flora and fauna; he needed to touch the earth again rather than concrete and brick, and so did Crazy Horse.

On these rides, Bogey told Lola stories about his home country of Colorado, about the mountains and plains, the rivers and creeks, about the wildlife and the seasons on the ranch, and about his family. Lola listened raptly to his tales, nearly unable to imagine such a vast, empty land and a life so different from her own. "I sure would like to see that some day," she murmured. "Why would you ever want to leave such a place to come here? It sounds like heaven to me." She was a good girl, Lola, and Bogey thought that he might be falling a little in love with her.

6

Finally, one afternoon in late October, a ship from France, the *Rochambeau,* put into port. Bogey went immediately down to the Harbor Master's office, where he was given the name of the ship's bursar, a Mr. Joubert, who was in charge of hiring.

At the ship's berth, a crew member conducted Bogey up the gangway and to the bursar's office. "Sit down, young man," said Mr. Joubert from behind his desk, indicating a chair. He was a tidy, elegant little fellow with pomaded black hair, dressed in a dark tailored suit and sporting a thin moustache. "I presume that you are here regarding a position on the crew?"

"Yes, sir, I come from the state of Colorado," Bogey said, "and I am going to France to join the Foreign Legion, to fight against the evil Huns."

At this, Mr. Joubert arched one eyebrow and jotted something on his notepad in exquisitely tiny handwriting. The bursar had small, manicured hands, and the precise manners of a veteran bureaucrat. "I see..." he said. "But Colorado is a great distance from the ocean, is it not?"

"Yes, sir, it is a real long way, that is for sure."

"And what experience do you have working on cargo vessels, young man?"

"None, sir. But I am a hard worker and a fast learner."

"Have you ever actually been on a ship before?" asked the bursar.

Bogey looked around the cabin. "No…no sir," he said, "I cannot say that I have. This would be my very first time. And I should mention, sir, that I have a horse who also requires transport for I intend to join the cavalry regiment of the Foreign Legion."

"Young man, I do not wish to disappoint you," said Mr. Joubert, "but the Foreign Legion does not have a cavalry regiment, only infantry."

"But that is impossible, sir," Bogey said. "I saw pictures of the French cavalry in the periodicals back home."

"Those would have been regular French Army Cavalry regiments, young man, not Foreign Legion."

"Well then, I will just have to join the French Army, won't I?"

"That, I'm afraid, is a right reserved only for French nationals," explained Mr. Joubert. "Hence the creation of the Legion itself, in order to allow non-nationals to fight for our country."

"But I do not wish to be a foot soldier," Bogey said. "You know what they say back home about a cowboy on foot, don't you sir?"

"Ah, no, I am quite sure that I do not know the answer to that question, young man," said Mr. Joubert.

"They say, 'if you're walking, you're not a real cowboy.'"

"This being the case," asked Mr. Joubert, "do you still wish transport for your horse to France?"

"I cannot very well leave him here, can I, sir?" said Bogey. "And it is too late now to send him home. I guess I will just have to find a place to stable him in France."

Mr. Joubert cleared his throat. "To the interview at hand, young man," he said, "do you know how to swim?"

"No, sir, I do not."

"As you have no previous experience at sea, what useful function do you believe you might be able to serve on the vessel?"

"I know how to fix things, sir," Bogey offered, "how to work with tools. I know how to take a tractor apart and put it back together again."

"Repairing tractors is not an especially useful talent on a cargo ship," said the bursar.

"No, sir, I do not suppose it would be," Bogey said, "but if you were to have engine trouble on the way home, I might be able to help out with that."

"But you see, young man, we have engineers aboard who perform such functions," said Mr. Joubert. "And how can I even be certain that, having never before been to sea, you would not be subject to seasickness? This late in the season, we frequently encounter violent storms, which can make for high seas and a very rough passage. It has happened in the past that inexperienced sailors have spent much of the voyage vomiting in buckets, which does not for a productive crew member make."

"Sir, back home I ride buckin' broncs in the rodeo," Bogey said, "you want to talk about a rough passage... Now, I been thrown plenty of times, it is true, but I have never once tossed my cookies."

Mr. Joubert did not know what a "buckin' bronc" was, nor did he have any idea what "thrown" or "tossed my cookies," meant. Yet somewhere beneath the bursar's chilly bureaucratic demeanor, there lurked a romantic in the finest French tradition, a spirit of nationalism which allowed him to secretly admire this bold young cowboy from Colorado, pursuing a wild dream of taking his horse to France to fight against the German invaders.

Plus, on a more practical and less altruistic level, the job with which Mr. Joubert had been charged by the ship's owners was to pay crew members the minimum wage possible, or better yet, pay them nothing at all.

For some time, Mr. Joubert tapped his pen briskly on his pad. "Young man," he finally said, nodding, "I believe that, indeed, I may be able to make room for you and your horse on the *Rochambeau.* However, as you have no previous experience at sea, and no demonstrable skills which might be useful to the ship, I can only offer you passage—food and a berth, as it were—for which you must work, without additional pay, and at whatever tasks, no matter how menial, the Captain and crew demand of you. You will, in short, be the lowliest crew member on board. At the same time, you will be responsible for providing a suitable enclosure in which to contain your horse securely in the hold, as well as sufficient feed for said animal for the duration of the voyage, which, depending on weather conditions, and the ultimate weight of our cargo, can take anywhere between ten to fourteen days. Due to predation by German submarines, we no longer put into port at Le Havre, but further south at Bordeaux, which makes the voyage that much longer, and is a still treacherous passage. Do you understand? And are you willing to accept these terms?"

"Yes, sir, Mister Joubert," Bogey answered. "I understand perfectly. I accept everything. I will work hard for you, and I won't let you or the Captain and crew down. You'll see, sir. Thank you."

Three weeks later, on Bogey's last night at Mona's, the girl Lola came to his room, slipped out of her clothes and lay down beside him. She whispered: "I don't want your last memory of this place to be of one of the girls, or several of them as you seem to prefer. I want it to be of me. I want you to carry my scent on the ship across the sea, all the way to France. I know that is the closest I will ever get to that country. Do you understand?"

Bogey nodded. He cupped her face in his hand, and looked into her eyes which shone in the light of a gas lamp on the table. She was light-haired and pale, and her skin was soft and smelled of the burning leaves of autumn drifting in the air, and when they made love it was different than with the other girls, whom Bogey did not love. He caressed her small breasts, which were like the breasts of a girl, and he kissed her hardened nipples, and when he entered her gently, they each knew that this was both the beginning of something, as well as the end, and that after this night they would never see each other again.

The *Rochambeau* sailed from the Port of New York at dawn on November 5, 1916, a gray, chilly morning with a light snow falling. As the tugboats detached their lines, and the ship entered the open sea, Bogey came up from below decks, where he had already been put to work scrubbing the crew's head. He stood at the railing and looked out at the monochrome sea and sky, which seemed welded together as if there were no horizon at all. Bogey thought that this vast, featureless ocean was just about the loneliest country he had ever in his life seen.

GABRIELLE

1918 - 1925

1

On a clear, cold January morning in 1925, 18-year-old Gabrielle Jungbluth left the Foyer des Jeunes Filles, a residence for young women students run by nuns of the Monastery of Visitation, on the rue Denfert-Rochereau in Montparnasse. She was off to attend her first day of art classes in the Atelier Humbert at Paris' prestigious L'École Nationale Supérieure des Beaux-Arts.

Gabrielle was a lovely girl, tall, long-legged and slender, with long black hair worn up under her wool hat, and large deep-set eyes that shined particularly brightly on this day. Her breath escaped in puffs of steam in the frigid morning air, and she walked with brisk purpose, carrying herself with a certain innate confidence that made her seem older than her years, her step at once strong and light, filled with all the wild faith of a precocious young painter, off to establish her claim on the world of art.

From the rue Denfert-Rochereau, Gabrielle crossed the boulevard Montparnasse, to the rue d'Assas, to the rue Guynemer, following the western border of the Luxembourg Gardens, gray and dormant in winter, the bony trees and distinguished statues dusted with snow fallen in the night. She crossed the rue Vaugirard, to the rue Bonaparte, passing the cathedral of Saint-Sulpice, across boulevard Saint-Germain, past the little church, regaining the rue Bonaparte, and arriving finally at

L'École des Beaux-Arts. It was a leisurely 25-minute walk, but with her long legs, determined stride, and in the excitement of the day, Gabrielle had covered it this first morning in nearly half that time.

The school ateliers opened onto the square cour du mûrier, a courtyard so named for the magnificent mulberry tree growing in its center, tall and straight, equally bare of leaves this time of year. As Gabrielle entered this rarefied space, she had the sense of traveling back to a time of antiquity, into a silent sanctuary of the arts where the noises of the modern city were muted by the stone arcades, the marble statues and majolicas. She might have been in ancient Italy, the Campo Santo of Pisa, or the Chiostro Verde of Florence. And yet for all its ornate elegance, she felt, too, the academic solemnity of the establishment, a certain institutional lack of joy.

Gabrielle had been here before in the course of her fall entrance examinations, and she had no trouble at all finding the Atelier Humbert. Although she believed she was arriving early, she saw that a number of other girls were already there, crowded around the door of the studio, reading a notice posted on the wall beside it.

"What is this you are looking at?" Gabrielle asked, jostling between the girls. "Let me see."

"It is the rules of the atelier," one of the girls answered. "And you don't have to be so rude, pushing between us like that. Everyone will have a chance to read it."

She laughed. "Yes, but I want to read it now." It was true that Gabrielle always wanted to be first, and in the future she planned to arrive here even earlier. "Regulations of the Atelier Humbert," she read at the top of the notice. "My goodness, such a lot of rules!"

"Forty-two articles, to be exact," said one of the other new girls in the atelier this semester. "But how shall we ever be able to remember them all?"

"Precisely why they are posted here," said one of the older students. "So that you may refer to them every day, until you have them memorized. And I suggest to you new girls that you begin writing them down in your notebooks. The professor is quite strict about his rules."

"I thought we came here to learn to paint," Gabrielle said, "not to be stenographers. I have no intention of writing these articles down in my notebook, and I am certainly not going to memorize them. You know what Picasso says about rules, don't you? He says that for the true artist rules are made to be broken."

From behind them came now the deep, authoritative voice of Professor Humbert himself. "Yes, he can say that because he is Picasso. But you, young lady, are not."

Gabrielle turned around, her cheeks reddening in the presence of the professor. "Excuse me, sir," she said. "I am very sorry. Please forgive me."

"You see, young lady, one is only allowed to break the rules after one has learned them," said Professor Humbert. "And that is why you are here. Mr. Picasso learned the rules of his craft, and absorbed the techniques of the masters quite early in his career. Now, for better or worse, he has chosen to abandon many of them, as has his friend, my former student, Mr. Braque. Now the two of them quite often paint nonsense, which will be forgotten as soon as the next popular movement comes along. However, they have earned the right to pursue whatever folly they wish. You, young lady, have not yet earned any such privilege, and, indeed, you may never do so. Study the rules of the atelier, write them down if necessary, and respect them. They are an important foundation to your success here. Anyone who chooses to ignore them will not long survive under my tutelage. Do I make myself clear?"

"Quite clear, sir, yes," Gabrielle answered.

The professor removed a keychain from his pocket, fumbled for a moment for the right key, then inserted it in the lock of the door and swung it open. "You may enter ladies," he said, "and for you new students, you may take your position behind any easel. As one of the articles of the *réglement* posted on the door states, when painting live models, we will be rotating positions so that all may benefit from different views and angles of the subject. Therefore, all positions are only temporary."

As Gabrielle stepped behind an easel, the older girl who had recommended memorizing the rules took the easel beside her. "Well done, young lady," she whispered smugly, "you are off to a fine start. It will clearly not be you who becomes the teacher's pet."

But Gabrielle had already recovered from her reprimand. She was behind an easel, in a real atelier, about to be instructed by a famous professor of art. Nothing could stop her now. "Ah, well," she answered to the girl, "we shall just see about that, won't we?"

2

Gabrielle's father, Colonel Charles Ismaël Jungbluth, was a veteran of the Great War, Commandeur de la Légion d'Honneur, *Croix de Guerre*, decorated for bravery in battle as Commandant of the 217th infantry. He was a distinguished looking man, small and wiry, with strong features and a large bushy black moustache, the ends twirled rakishly upwards, as if in a kind of whimsical smile, which however, did not conceal the colonel's rather intimidating demeanor.

Yet Colonel Jungbluth had a softer side as well, and it was from her father that Gabrielle had inherited both her talent and her interest in painting, for he was a gifted amateur painter himself. From the time that she had been a little girl, he had taken his only child out with him into the fields, forests and mountains to paint *en plein air*, his preferred style.

Despite her own mischievous nature, and the fact that the colonel ran the household with a certain militaristic authority, Gabrielle adored her father, and he her, and both had learned to accept the fact that they had very different, yet oddly complementary temperaments. She was an impish little girl, who had inherited equally of both her parents' physical beauty, a healthy measure of her father's strength of character, and all of her mother's *joie de vivre.* Thirteen years younger than her husband, Marie-Reine Jungbluth, was a gay, stylish woman who sometimes chafed under the stern rule of the colonel, but who largely accepted it as the status quo of married life in that era. Her daughter was another matter. So full of life and energy, and an innate spirit of rebellion and stubbornness, Gabrielle was not afraid, even at a young age, to stand up to her father, and was almost always able to coax a laugh from the dour-faced colonel. They had a fine time together on their painting excursions.

The Jungbluth family lived at the time outside the city of Epinal, in the Vosges, and it was there in the company of her father, who always wore a jauntily cocked beret when he went out with his easel, that Gabrielle learned the joy of the creative process. Yet her own artistic interests would lie more in depicting people, than the landscapes of her father, which was another trait she shared with her far more sociable mother.

At the outbreak of the war, the colonel had installed his wife and daughter in an apartment in Paris, as the Vosges was directly in the path of the advancing German army. And at the end of the war, the family moved to a house in the country outside the city of Rouen.

As all who came home from the front, Colonel Jungbluth had witnessed much death and devastation during the war, had seen vast swaths of the verdant countryside of northern France decimated by the sheer tonnage of bombs rained upon it, poisoning the soil, turning it into a charred wasteland uninhabitable by man, flora or fauna. When the fighting was finally over and he returned to his wife and daughter, all the colonel had wished to do was to escape into the surviving countryside, and to paint again, as if by creating his little pastoral landscapes, he could in some way help to heal the broken earth.

Gabrielle was only 11-years-old upon her father's return, but she had kept painting and drawing on her own while he had been away at war, in part simply as a means of keeping him safe. In her child's mind, as long as she was working in the private world of art they shared, and would have something new to show him when he came home, her beloved papa could not be harmed. Now when they went out together, Gabrielle carried her own sketchpad, and when the colonel looked at her efforts, as juvenile as they still were, he recognized that his daughter already possessed a natural talent far greater than his own.

Like so many veterans who survived the war, Colonel Jungbluth did not speak of those terrible times. But Gabrielle was a curious child, a perpetual seeker of truth, one who wanted to know all about everything, and who never ceased asking questions. When they went out painting again, she pestered her father for stories about the war, about the places he had been, and the people he had met. "Did you kill very many *Boches*, Papa?" she asked.

"You are too young for stories of killing, my child," answered the colonel, "while I am too old, and have seen too much of it, to tell such tales. Although they were our enemies, you must also remember that we have deep ancestral roots in Germany, and our native territory of Alsace has been at various times a part of that country. And you must remember, too, that the boys the Germans sent to the front, were young men just like our own, with families—brothers and sisters, mothers and fathers and grandparents—waiting for them to come home, and with the same hopes and dreams for their futures. Often these so-called "soldiers" were little older than children themselves. Other than doing one's duty to one's country, I can assure you that there is no honor, and certainly no pleasure in the killing of children."

"Why do we have wars then, Papa?" Gabrielle asked. "Does anything good ever come out of them?"

The colonel considered this question for some time. "War is at base the most barbaric of human enterprises," he answered finally, "though it can also sometimes bring liberty from tyranny. And it can bring out both the best as well as the worst in people. Sometimes one witnesses acts of great kindness, mercy, sacrifice, and courage. And sometimes in such circumstances, one has occasion to meet extraordinary people. Perhaps that is the good that comes out of war."

"Then tell me a story about such an act, or about such a person," Gabrielle said.

"Your curiosity is incorrigible, my daughter," said the colonel. "Why do you want your father to relive a time he only wishes to forget?"

"But you don't want to forget the good as well as the bad, do you, father?" she asked. "I want to hear a good story about an act of kindness, mercy, sacrifice, and courage. Or about one of the extraordinary people you met."

The colonel laughed then and shook his head. "Alright, my child, I am going to indulge you, for it is true that one cannot be a good artist unless one is curious about life and about people. But let me think for a moment while we paint, of a war story that is suitable for a young girl's ears. And you, stop asking me questions for a moment and concentrate on your own drawing."

So father and daughter worked for a while in silence, seated side by side on the banks of the River Seine, she sketching and he painting. Some time passed in this way, with only the sounds of the summer birds singing, the murmur of the river, the scratch of Gabrielle's colored pencils against her sketchpad, and the softer whispers of her father's brush on canvas.

3

"I shall never forget that terrible day," the colonel began, finally. "April 17, 1917, the second day of General Nivelle's disastrous spring offensive along the Chemin des Dames. The Germans were ready for us, and my regiment was pinned down in hastily-dug trenches in the hills outside Champagne, under attack by a savage barrage of machine gun fire and mortar shelling. The chaos of a major artillery assault is impossible to imagine, or to describe...the deafening blasts, the air thick with smoke and dirt, the screams of the wounded and dying. Already some of our troops were beginning to mutiny, dropping their weapons and running for their lives through the hills. And before the ill-advised campaign was finally called off after three days, many, many more would desert. General Pétain would later order 400 of our own terrified boys to be executed for desertion. All but 40 were finally spared by military tribunals—nevertheless, not only did the Germans kill our soldiers, but we, too, killed them. This is the madness, the barbarity of war, my daughter, that we execute our own children simply because they were afraid to die.

"It would become known as *La Bataille des Monts,* and I shall spare you further details of the butchery that day, for within the midst of this horror, I am going to relate to you the *'good'* war story which you seek. Although you can perhaps begin to understand how difficult it is to separate the good from the bad in any story of war, and why I do not wish to speak of that time." The colonel paused then for a moment as if still constructing a suitable version of his story.

"So heavy was the machine gun fire at times that day," he continued, "that we dared not raise our heads above the trenches. But during a lull in the action, one of my men called out, 'Look there, on the ridge to the east!' And when we looked, we saw a man on horseback galloping toward us across the hills. Artillery shells exploded around him, and the earth was kicked up by the machine gun bullets, and yet on he rode, unscathed. This was no normal horseman, at least not like any we had ever before seen. He rode a pale grey horse but he did not appear to be an allied soldier as he was not dressed in military uniform, nor did he have a standard issue military saddle. We watched him in silence, and with a growing sense of wonder as he rode toward us, somehow evading shells and bullets. Later, when we had a chance to compare our impressions, we found that we all had the same strange sensation…that we had already died in battle, and had been somehow transported to another front, in a distant land, in a different time, for as the horseman drew closer, it was more than ever clear that he was not a soldier, at least no regular soldier."

The colonel paused here, and set his brush down on the easel. He smiled, remembering. "And he was certainly not a Frenchman…"

"Well, what was he then, Papa?" Gabrielle asked, impatiently. "Who was he?"

"A cowboy," said the colonel. "He was an American cowboy riding right out of the old West, like a character in the moving pictures."

"A cowboy!" Gabrielle shrieked with delight.

"Now our men began to cheer him on as he raced across no-man's land," her father continued, "he and his horse sometimes disappearing into the billows of smoke and blasted earth from the artillery explosions all around them, but then miraculously reappearing again, galloping inexorably from the clouds as if out of a dream. The Germans had constructed a barricade of barbed wire and downed trees to defend their position from attack, and, incredibly, over this the cowboy's horse now sailed, as if it had the ability of flight. As you know, my dear, I have a good deal of equestrian experience, but never, before or since, have I witnessed anything like this remarkable feat of horsemanship. Gaining our bivouac, the cowboy swung nimbly from the saddle, and led his mount down into our trench.

Rising from my position, I went to meet him. He was a tall, handsome young fellow, wearing a tattered, stained cowboy hat, and those leather leggings that American cowboys wear over their pants, "chaps," they are called. And, of course, he wore cowboy boots. He also carried a western six-shooter in a holster strapped to his hip, a Colt .45, I later learned. I approached him, with my own firearm drawn as a precaution, for we could not know who he was, or what his mission; indeed, perhaps he was a Trojan horse, sent by the Germans themselves to infiltrate our position.

"Identify yourself!" I demanded.

The cowboy saluted me, and said in very rudimentary French: 'No need for the weapon, sir. I am Legionnaire 2nd Class Lambert, sir, of the 4th Battalion under the command of Colonel Jacques Daumier. I am the colonel's courier, sir, and I bring you a classified dispatch.'

"'If you are truly a legionnaire, then why are you not in uniform, soldier?' I asked.

"'By special permission of the colonel, sir,' he answered. 'In order to deliver this communication as fast as possible, I crossed our own lines into territory held by the enemy. I suggested to the colonel that I thought it might confuse the *Boches*, maybe even scare them a little, sir, if they saw a cowboy riding behind their lines.'

"My daughter, when one is in the trenches on the front," said the colonel, "under fire by machine guns and heavy artillery, with men dying all around, I cannot tell you how rare it is that one has occasion to laugh. But when the boy said this, and in such an ingenuous manner, I began laughing. And when I called out his words to my men in the trenches, and they, in turn, relayed them down the line, *'A legionnaire, a courier, American. He thought it might confuse the Boches if they saw a cowboy riding behind their lines'*, all started laughing.

"This perplexed the boy, 'Why does everybody laugh, sir?' he asked me. 'Is it my poor French?'

"'No, no, not at all,' I answered. 'But, you see, Legionnaire Lambert, it also rather confused *us* to see a cowboy riding behind enemy lines. If I may ask you, young man, how in the world have you managed to avoid being captured or killed on this mission?'

"The legionnaire seemed to consider this for a moment, as though the question had never before occurred to him, and then he answered: 'Well sir, all I can say is that I have a real good horse, a fine sense of direction, and the two of us have always had pretty darned good luck in life.'

"The boy stayed with us in our position for several hours, waiting for nightfall and a lull in the shelling before leaving to return to his regiment. He spoke of his country, his home, his parents' ranch in Colorado. Such a fine young man. He told us that he had come to France the year before in order to join the Foreign Legion. And do you know why?"

Gabrielle shook her head.

"For no other reason than the fact that his parents had told him their family had French blood," the colonel said. "He wished to help defend the country of his ancestors. You see, my child, how foolish young men are? He came all the way from the state of Colorado. And he brought his horse with him because he thought that he could join the cavalry regiment. But, of course, the Foreign Legion does not have a cavalry regiment..." the colonel paused, shaking his head at the foolishness of young men.

"Nevertheless, young Lambert did join the Legion," her father continued, "the infantry regiment, to be sure. He took basic training in Perpignan, and he stabled his horse on a farm there. He was a strong boy and because he grew up in country of high elevation, he was always in the lead on training marches through the Pyrenees. Indeed, he was a born leader in many ways, and he quickly impressed his superiors with his intelligence and competence. In times of leisure, the officers had also witnessed the young man's extraordinary equestrian skills.

"Because we so desperately needed soldiers on the front at the time, basic training was foreshortened, and the boy's regiment sent up in only a few short weeks. Even though the Legion had no cavalry, of course many of their officers had horses, as did we regular Army officers. As you know, I had my beloved Caracol with me throughout the war. Legionnaire Lambert convinced one of his lieutenant colonels to take his horse to the front with the rest of the staff's mounts. And so as not to risk losing one of their valuable officers for what was an especially hazardous duty, young Lambert was pressed into service as a courier. And that is how he happened to ride into our bivouac on that day. I asked him how on earth his horse had been able to leap the German barbed wire barricade, and he told me that as a boy he had grown tired of dismounting to open gates on his family's ranch, and so he had trained his horse to jump the barbed wire fences—which, of course, did not begin to explain the magnitude of the leap we had witnessed.

"When darkness fell, the boy remounted his horse and galloped off as he had come. From that time forward, Legionnaire 2nd Class Lambert, would become known as the 'cowboy courier,' and it is my understanding that even the Germans came to call him that.

"We were never to see him again after that night, but young Lambert became rather a legendary figure on the front, undertaking many dangerous missions, delivering communiqués back-and-forth between the Legionnaires, the regular French Army regiments, the British troops, as well as those of the Americans, who had just entered the war. It was true that he was considered to have special powers of good fortune, as if divinely protected. Many stories were told of his heroic exploits, and although these were surely exaggerated, he was nevertheless an inspiring figure to men on the front. In the most desperate times of war, simply the idea of such romantic characters can bring great solace to exhausted, frightened troops. As the cowboy courier's fame spread up and down the front, none of the

German soldiers wanted to be the one to shoot him, for fear that it would bring bad luck down upon them. It was as if he had a kind of unwritten, unspoken pass to see him through the war."

"What was the boy's first name, Papa?" Gabrielle asked.

"Bogart. Bogart Lambert," said the colonel, "which you see, my daughter, is another small irony of this story, for the first name "Bogart" is both an old-French name, as well as an old-German one, and it is entirely possible that the ancestors of whom he spoke may also, like our family, have had Alsatian roots."

"And what was the name of his horse?"

"Crazy Horse."

"That's a funny name!"

"Yes, named evidently after a famous American Indian chief," said the colonel. "Well, then, there is your good war story, my daughter. Now let us concentrate on our art, shall we?"

"But what became of the cowboy courier, finally, Papa?" Gabrielle asked. "How does the story end?"

A shadow passed across the colonel's face. "It ends with the young American cowboy, galloping away from our bivouac into the darkness of night, lit only by the occasional flash of exploding artillery shells. I told you, I never saw the boy again, I only heard tales of him. That is the end of the story. We shall now paint the river in peace, and in silence."

"I am no longer drawing the river, Papa," she said. "I am drawing the cowboy, Bogart Lambert, and his horse, Crazy Horse. Look." She held her sketchpad out to him.

"Very nice," said the colonel. "However, as you have only seen him in your imagination, I can help you with a few authentic details. For instance, tied to his western saddle, the boy also carried a coiled rope, which, he explained to us, he used in rodeo competitions back home."

"He died, didn't he, Papa?" Gabrielle asked. "The *Boches* killed him, after all, didn't they? I can tell from your face."

As if he had not heard her, the colonel busied himself mixing oils on his palette. Finally, he turned to his daughter. "*That,* my daughter, is the end of the story."

4

The next few years after the war passed quickly and happily for Gabrielle and her family. Summers vacations were spent at the beach in Dieppe, with periodic trips to Paris made during the rest of the year in order that they might benefit from exposure to the art and culture there, pursuits not so readily available in the provinces. The family visited the museums and the exhibitions, and Gabrielle and her mother went shopping in the chic districts.

But what fascinated the girl most was the time they spent in Montparnasse, which the colonel, too, enjoyed visiting due to his own interest in the art world. The quarter seemed to be its own separate enclave from the rest of Paris. Indeed, longtime residents referred to it simply as the "village," a place with its own distinct atmosphere, a kind of crazed energy that had been suppressed by the years of war, only to explode now like an uncorked champagne bottle, spraying in celebration of liberation, a new way of expression, a new way of being—the rebirth and reinvention of both life and art.

Infected by this artistic ebullience, which seemed to hang over the city like a sensual red mist, Gabrielle begged her father for the chance to study painting there. Although Colonel Jungbluth did not always approve of the direction the modern art world was taking, he could not ignore his daughter's innate talent, and the fact that, for better or worse, she clearly already owned the soul of an artist. He also recognized that as a strictly amateur painter himself, he had taught the girl everything he could. And so the colonel encouraged Gabrielle to begin practicing and studying for the stringent entrance examinations to *L'Atelier Humbert.* In so doing, Colonel Jungbluth also understood that he would be sending her off to fulfill secret, and unrealized, artistic dreams of his own.

As usual, the Jungbluth family spent the month of August, 1924, at the beach, and it was during this same summer that Gabrielle seemed to blossom almost overnight from gawky adolescence into young womanhood. Her long legs, which had previously owned a kind of awkward, coltish quality, took on a new more mature shape and form, and her long confident stride and the natural way in which she swung her hips when she walked, caused men's heads to turn on the boardwalk. Her full red lips and warm flashing smile seduced people with a kind of instinctive innocence, and when focused upon an individual, made one feel in that moment like the most important person on earth. She wore her thick black hair piled upon her head, and when released from her bathing cap, it spilled halfway down her back. And her dark, deep-set eyes suggested a certain wisdom beyond her years, the impenetrable mystery that sometimes resides in the hearts of artists.

And so it was in the fall of that year, that Gabrielle Odile Rosalie Jungbluth, had arrived in Paris and taken lodging arranged by her father at Le Foyer des Jeunes Filles on the rue Denfert-Rochereau in Montparnasse. The atelier of classicist painter and longtime professor, Jacques Ferdinand Humbert, was the first and only of its kind for women, and as such there was great competition for the limited number of coveted spaces available. As she was not enrolled at L'École des Beaux-Arts itself, Gabrielle was applying to the Atelier Humbert as a "*élève libre*"(free student), for which there were even fewer openings. The professor himself would choose these students, based upon whatever criterion he wished, and he had devised a series of tests which required applicants to draw designs in studios on the premises of the school, in three different disciplines: anatomy, perspective, and portraiture.

Gabrielle had been the youngest applicant that semester, but she had a particular talent for rendering the human form. And in the results of her tests, Professor Humbert recognized not only a certain technical skill, however raw and unrefined, but also something deeper, something he was less able to qualify or define, but which he had seen in a handful of his students over the decades, including the young George Braque. Had he been able to articulate this specific quality, what he saw in the young Jungbluth girl's efforts was a fundamental strength of character, an artistic point of view informed by genuine passion. And this was enough in Humbert's mind to choose Gabrielle as one of his students over a dozen other more technically proficient applicants. Her work was simply bolder, franker, and more interesting.

5

Perhaps because her parents never had a son, nor Gabrielle brothers to teach her otherwise, she had grown up believing that she was the equal of any boy. Yet this was clearly not the prevailing cultural attitude of the time toward girls, nor that of either the state or L'École des Beaux-Arts. Indeed, not until the year 1896, had women even been allowed to use the school library and to attend lectures in the school conference halls, and not until the following year had they been accepted as full students. And it was 1900 before aspiring women painters were finally provided with an atelier of their own. Yet fully a quarter century later, when Gabrielle began studying under Professor Humbert, women were still prohibited, on the grounds of "impropriety," from studying in the numerous ateliers open to men.

As a "free student," Gabrielle was allowed access to the school library, and frequently after class in the atelier she did reading there on the subjects of art history and painting in general, as required by Professor Humbert, who also periodically asked his students to write essays on various topics.

One afternoon while Gabrielle was in the library researching an essay to submit to the professor on a topic she herself had chosen, a boy came to her table and sat down beside her.

"What is that you are working on there mademoiselle?" the boy whispered.

"None of your business," Gabrielle said.

"I am Adrian Fleury," said the boy with a certain flourish, as if his name was already known in the art world. "I am a student here. I am going to be a great sculptor."

"I'm happy for you," she said. "But I'm busy, please leave me alone."

"And you?"

"And me, what?"

"Who are you?"

"I am a student in the Atelier Humbert."

"Ah, yes, of course you are, the girl's class," the boy said dismissively. He leaned over proprietarily to look at Gabrielle's notebook. "'The History of Women Painters in the Art World'," he read. "Well, that is certain to be a short essay, isn't it?"

"Why would you say such a thing?" she asked.

"Because everyone knows how few accomplished woman artists there have been throughout history. And most of those are lesbians. Clearly, the female gender in general has never had a great facility for painting or sculpture, or, for that matter, for literature. You are simply not gifted in those ways."

"And in what ways, then, in your opinion, are we gifted?" Gabrielle asked.

"Historically," said the boy, "the most important function women have served is as muses for male artists."

"Ah, yes, to pose as models, clean your studios, wash your brushes, and to perform various other services, is that correct?"

"Exactly so."

"Which is precisely the thesis of my essay," said Gabrielle. "That throughout the course of history, women have been denied access to instruction in the arts. If such pursuits are largely closed to us, how then are we to have developed the facility of which you speak?"

"I would like you to come to my atelier to model for me," said the boy, as if he had not heard a word of what she had said. "I will immortalize you in clay."

"And would you like me to pose nude for you?"

"But of course, that is precisely what I had in mind."

Gabrielle laughed. "You are a bit of an egotistical fool, aren't you?"

"I beg your pardon?"

"I would not consider posing for you, either nude or fully dressed," she said. "I am a painter, not a model. Please leave me alone now."

In this way, in her very first semester at the atelier, Gabrielle Jungbluth began already to gain a bit of a reputation among students and faculty as a troublemaker, an agitator, an anarchist, a feminist and quite possibly, a lesbian, although, to be sure, she had also some like-minded friends and supporters. L'École des Beaux-Arts and its associated ateliers, were still very much institutions of the establishment, run by male academics who held on stubbornly to the entrenched beliefs of the previous century that women were to be tolerated, placated when necessary, but largely ignored.

Nevertheless, Professor Humbert took great pride in his women students, although only a small handful had gone on to viable careers as artists in the quarter-century during which he had been teaching his atelier at Beaux-Arts. He was a demanding teacher, bad tempered, quick to anger and harsh in his judgments, and he brought some of his students to tears with his diatribes against their style, their technique, their lack of talent. But no matter how severe the criticisms the professor leveled toward her own work, Gabrielle remained sanguine, and she would never cry for him. In addition to her innate self-confidence, her father, the colonel was, after all, a career military man, and she had learned from him a certain stoicism. Too proud to cry, she was damned if she would give Humbert the satisfaction of behaving like a member of the "weaker sex." Instead, she met his attacks with a small inscrutable smile, which she noticed even managed to disconcert the professor.

Despite his occasional harshness, Gabrielle understood that she had much to learn about the fundamentals of painting from Professor Humbert. Although he was resistant to change, as is so often the nature of old men, and inflexible in his ideas and methods, she came to appreciate his honesty of critique and his insistence on exactitude. He clearly cared deeply about his atelier, and Gabrielle was determined to be an attentive student, to work harder at her craft than any of the others.

For his part, Professor Humbert had long since given up any illusions that he would be remembered by posterity as a great artist. He was certainly a fine classical painter, more than competent, but without that spark of genius required to transcend a certain mediocrity. As he entered the last decade of his life and career, Humbert came to realize that he was far more likely to be remembered as a teacher rather than a painter. He had been working at his profession long enough to know that genius was an elusive quality, and even then not always a sufficient one to ensure success. Indeed, some of his most naturally-gifted students over the long span of his career, had come to nothing, lacking, finally, some other elusive component—drive or tenacity, or simply the requisite faith in themselves and in the value of their work. For every Georges Braque he had instructed, there had been a thousand who may at first have appeared to hold equal promise, only to vanish into obscurity.

Over the decades, the professor had developed a nearly infallible ability to identify early on those students who had the best chance to achieve genuine artistic careers. As he worked with young Gabrielle Jungbluth, he came to see increasingly not only that she possessed the necessary raw talent, but also a certain lust for art that seemed to own a kind of sensual manifestation. And he knew that this had been his own missing component. It is sometimes the unconscious impulse of old academics, who have long since given up their artistic dreams, to wish to dampen or even extinguish such fires within their students. In nearly every class there was at least one troublemaker, one who pushed against his authority and rebelled against conventions, and Professor Humbert could see that this year it would clearly be the Jungbluth girl who would require his firmest hand.

BOGEY

1918 - 1924

1

Just before dawn on the morning of November 11th, 1918, Legionnaire 1st Class Bogart Lambert (promoted to that rank due to his splendid service to the Foreign Legion) was traveling north from the battlefield in Mézière, France on the road to Mons, Belgium.

Bogey had ridden half the previous day and all night under a half moon, carrying a dispatch to the commanders of the British and American forces, notifying them that after four years the Somme had finally been retaken. Winter was coming on, a cold drizzle began to fall, and Bogey put on the old canvas long rider coat he once wore while checking cattle during rainy season back home, one-hundred years ago it seemed now.

Yet it had been only two years since Bogey first arrived in France, and over a year and a half since he had been on the front, and he was no longer an ingenuous boy with romantic visions of the glory of war, but a battle-hardened veteran soldier who had witnessed all that was horrifying in the human impulse to slaughter one another. He had written stories in his notebooks about his experiences, and these he left with a friend back at his regiment whenever he was on a mission. He did not know what he would do with his stories when the war was over, and he wondered when he went back home, how he could even begin to tell his family and friends what it had really been like here. What possible good could it do to tell them the truth? He had written many letters home during the past two years, but as the war wore on and the devastation mounted, his own spirit declined commensurately, and words had begun to fail him. He finally determined that the language of war could not be articulated in prose, but only expressed in sound—the percussive boom of launched shells, the whine of incoming artillery, the crash of explosions and rattle of machine gun fire, and as a constant refrain to these brutal noises of carnage, the screams of the wounded and dying.

Bogey pulled his hat brim down and his collar up against the icy rain, which was turning to a wet snow. Although the sun had not yet risen, the horizon was already lit by the morning bombardment. He wondered if there would be yet another winter of war, he wondered if the war would ever end, he wondered if he would ever get back home. After all he had seen, that time and place seemed like a distant mirage now, and his own youth on the ranch like a vague memory of someone else's life.

He rode slowly this morning for Crazy Horse had thrown a shoe in the night and come up lame, and they were both exhausted. They rode through the blackened wasted no-man's land of dead trees, shell craters, abandoned trenches, and barbed wire, a poisoned earth that had been under siege for four years, and upon which nothing could grow, not a single weed. It was country that could make a man lose all hope, a land of howling ghosts stinking of death. This is not war, Bogey thought, this is the end of the world. He did not know whether or not he believed in hell, but if such a place existed, he imagined that it must be just like this, and he hoped that he would never have to go there again.

As the sky began to lighten to the east, Bogey tried to remember how the meadows at home had looked during the fall haying season, with the teams of draft horses in the fields, the mounds of still green grass, the fine rich smells of man and horse sweat and fresh-cut hay. He remembered that when he was a young boy his job was to take a wagon down to the creek in the morning with his friend Clarence, the neighbor's son, and the two of them would catch trout until they had filled the whole wagon, and then his mother would fry them up to feed the hay crew for lunch. And in the days after haying season, Bogey remembered how the cut fields turned golden with the advancing fall, and the aspen trees in the mountains went orange and red and yellow. He thought if only he could hold theses images of the changing seasons in his mind, of a world of growth and renewal when one year was much like the next, that he just might be able to maintain some measure of his sanity.

The road to Mons was oddly deserted, strangely silent but for the deep rumble of war in the distance, like a far-away thunderstorm. The Allied armies here, too, had pushed the front further north and east, driving the Germans back the way they had come. As so many who go to war begin to ask, Bogey wondered what was the point of it all? All these dead men, all this ruined earth, so that finally those who have survived can go home the way they have come.

Now Bogey heard overhead the heavy whoosh of beating wings, and even before he looked up, he recognized the sound as a familiar one he knew from home, and when he raised his head to the sky, he was heartened to see a single crow flying above him, another living thing with whom to share this cold, bleak dawn. And as crows often do in a certain spirit of sociability, the bird cawed to him in greeting as it flew over, and Bogey cawed back to him as he used to at home.

In that very instant, as the crow looked down upon man and horse, and the man looked up and cawed at him, an enormous explosion detonated beneath them, a black cloud of smoke, earth, shrapnel, flesh, blood and bone billowing in the air, obscuring them from his sight, the crow himself lifted by the sudden surge of hot air rising. Banking sharply off to avoid being struck himself by flying shards, the crow cawed again, angrily this time, he too, tired of witnessing so much death, so much human folly. He flew on.

2

It was springtime, and he was at one end of an irrigation ditch culvert on the ranch, and someone was speaking to him from the other end, it must be his father, but the voice was so faint, so far away that he could not make out the words, only the hollow echo of them. “Is that you, Daddy?” he asked, “I can’t hear you? What are you doing down in the culvert? Talk louder, I can’t hear you.”

“Can you hear me now?” said the voice, and it wasn’t his father, after all, but a stranger’s voice. “Can you understand what I am saying to you?”

Bogey opened his eyes then and looked up into a man’s face. “Who are you?” he asked.

“I am Dr. Fergus MacLeod,” said the man. “And who are you?”

“I am Bogart Lambert,” he said.

“Excellent!” said the doctor. “You have been here with us for quite some time, Mr. Lambert, and I am very pleased to meet you at last. How are you feeling?”

“Where am I?”

“The Edinburgh War Hospital in Edinburgh, Scotland, Mr. Lambert.”

“Why? How did I get here?”

“Can you tell me what nationality you are?”

“I’m American.”

“Splendid!” said the doctor. “And can you tell me why you were in France?”

"I'm not answering any more of your questions until you tell me why I am here and how I got here." Bogey said.

"Fair enough, Mr. Lambert," said the doctor, "but you see I am only trying to establish your mental state. You have been severely wounded, and in-and-out of consciousness for over four months. This is the first time you have been responsive, the first time you have spoken. You were involved in a serious explosion in a theatre of war on the border between France and Belgium. You were found there by Scottish troops traveling to the front. Are you understanding everything I am saying to you, Mr. Lambert?"

"Yes."

"Excellent. You had no identification on your person when they came upon you. Indeed, you were practically naked, virtually all your clothes had been blown off your body. You would have died from your wounds and from exposure to the weather had the troops not discovered you when they did. You see, all this time we have had no way of knowing your identity, your nationality, or what you were doing on the front."

"How do I know you are who you say you are?" asked Bogey. "How do I know you aren't the enemy and this isn't a trick?"

Dr. Macleod laughed. "Considering the extent of your injuries, Mr. Lambert," he said, "and the long duration of your semi-comatose state, your mind is functioning with remarkably acuity. When I come to see you next, I will bring the credentials necessary to confirm my identity. More immediately, you will perhaps notice from my accent that I am not German."

"Is the war over, doctor?"

"Yes."

"Did we win?"

The doctor hesitated and looked down. "Yes, we won," he said sadly, "if one can call such terrible cost a victory."

"What is the date today?" Bogey asked.

"March 23, 1919," said the doctor.

"And when did the war end?"

"Officially, the Armistice was signed at 11:00 am on November 11, roughly fours hours after you were found by our troops. However, word of this did not reach the front lines until some time later. As a result, many additional fatalities occurred among all of our armies on that final day. Now may I ask you one more question, Mr. Lambert?"

Bogey nodded.

"What is the very last thing you remember?"

Bogey considered this for some time.

"The crow," he whispered, finally, "I remember the crow." Suddenly, panicked, Bogey tried to sit up, but he found that he was too weak, could barely raise his head from the pillow. "Where is Crazy Horse?"

Dr. Macleod took him gently by the shoulders. "Please, you must not strain yourself."

"Where is my horse?"

The doctor shook his head. "Your horse absorbed the full-force of the explosion," he said. "Evidently he stepped on what was either a land mine, or an unexploded artillery shell. We are still removing pieces of shrapnel from your body, as well as shards of horse bone. Your horse's bulk saved your life, but he died instantly. You were thrown twenty feet away by the force of the blast."

Bogey started weeping, and he tried to turn his head away, embarrassed to break down like this in front of the doctor. "I'm sorry, but Crazy Horse was all I had left," he said.

"Mr. Lambert," said Dr. Fergus Macleod, "I, too, am truly sorry for you. But thanks to your horse, you have your whole life left."

"I guess our luck finally ran out," Bogey said, as if to himself.

"Believe me, young man," said the doctor, "you have no idea how lucky you are."

"Doctor?"

"Yes, Mr. Lambert."

"Today is my 20th birthday."

"Ah! Well then, you see, you have received a fine gift!"

3

Dear Mama and Daddy,

I suppose the Foreign Legion informed you of my presumed death some months ago, and I am sorry to have worried you so. By now you will have received the telegram from the doctor, telling you that I am not dead after all. I guess you also know that I'm in the war hospital in Edinburgh, Scotland. My brave old boy Crazy Horse saved my life, but he was killed. They say we stepped on a landmine or maybe a live shell. Whichever it was, it blew me right out of the saddle, and blew Crazy Horse all to Hell (sorry to use a cuss word Mama, but that's just how it was.) I guess I still carry some pieces of his bone around in my legs and somehow I kind of like that notion, as if he's become a part of me now.

I don't know exactly why, but I haven't told them here at the hospital that I was in the Legion, and I'd just as soon you didn't tell them, either. I pretend I don't remember. They see a lot of that around here. I guess I just want to be left alone until I get better. I was hurt pretty bad in the explosion, but I'm getting stronger every day. The doctor says I'm going to be here for a long time getting rehabilitated, with more surgeries to come, maybe as long as a year, or even longer. I still feel like I'm a little dead…I have a good deal of numbness and nerve pain in my arms and legs, and I have no muscles left at all. The doctor says I was mostly unconscious for over four months, and that it's going to take some time for me to get back to something close to normal, although he made it clear that I'll never get all the way there. But I've already started to walk a little on my own, and as soon as I get stronger, I'm going to start boxing again. I'm so skinny now you wouldn't recognize me. I hardly recognize myself when I look in the mirror. And I'm so darned weak that I couldn't go one round in the ring with a newborn kitten.

Everyone has been real nice to me here, and from what little I can see out the window of my room, the country is awful pretty, about like the country east of Boulder in the spring on a good wet year. As it looks like I'm going to be here for a long time, maybe I'll start writing stories again, just to help pass the time. If I do, I'll send some home to you. I don't know what happened to my notebooks with all my old stories in them. I left them with a legionnaire friend, a fellow from Tennessee named Fred Dunn, and when I never came back, I'll bet he threw them away. But that's OK, I wouldn't blame Fred for that, because they weren't worth much anyway and I don't think anyone would even care to read them.

When they found me, they had no way of knowing who I was. If I had died, which the doctor said by all rights I should have, I would have been buried in an unknown soldier's grave on the front, and no one would have ever known what had become of me. I imagine that's what the Legion wrote to you, and I am awful sorry for the worry it must have caused you. It is a real strange feeling, I can tell you, to die and come back to life again, and to remember the life part, but not the dying.

Speaking of that Mama, I don't have any clothes, and I'm mighty tired of wearing nothing but hospital gowns. The nurses like to tease me when I'm in the hallway with my walker, and my skinny butt is showing. But I give it right back to them, you can bet on that. So maybe you could send me a couple of snap-button shirts, and a pair or two of Levis? Just get my regular size and I'll grow back into them. That will give me some way of judging how I'm coming along. And please don't forget to send a belt, maybe the one with my old rodeo buckle that I left up in my room. And also a pair of good boots, please, and a hat. I lost everything when we got blown up. Everything.

I don't know when I'll be home again. When I get out of the hospital and finish with my rehabilitation, I may stay here for a while. Or maybe I'll go back to France for a time. For some reason I can't really explain right now, I feel like I have some unfinished business there. I know that you are going to want to come see me over here, but that you don't have the money for the trip. And I know you both have to look after the ranch and the cattle. All that is OK, really, I understand, I want you to know that. Even if you could, I wouldn't want you to come now, I wouldn't want you to see me like this. But I'm going to get strong again, and one day after I get a few things settled in my own head, I'll come home. I promise. In the meantime, I'll keep writing to you, and please write me back with news from home. Do you have good snow pack in the high country this year? I'll bet you've already started calving. I sure hope the weather holds out good for you.

Your loving son, back from the dead,
Bogart

4

And so Bogey began the long road to recovery. His legs had suffered the most trauma in the explosion, and over a period of ten more months the surgeons performed seven additional operations, removing more shrapnel and bone shards and trying to repair damaged muscle, tissue, and tendons.

As Bogey began gradually to regain strength and improved ability to walk, the hospital moved him into a separate building that housed wounded veterans where he continued his therapy. When he saw some of the men there missing arms or legs, or both, and others who suffered from permanent shell shock, and sat all day staring blankly into the middle-distance, and yet others so terribly disfigured that they barely resembled human beings any longer, he stopped feeling sorry for himself, and began to think that maybe his luck hadn't run out after all.

Bogey worked hard to build up his body again, making progress that further surprised the doctors. After an additional thirteen months, they allowed him to start light training at a private boxing gym, where he also began to work part time. In June of 1921, following two years of surgery and rehabilitation, the hospital finally released him.

The owner of the gym, a retired lightweight Scotsman by the name of Archie Munro, took Bogey under his wing, giving him work in return for free training, and also letting him move into a small flat above the gym.

Archie liked the young American, saw promise in his boxing skills, and as part of the training process, began arranging sparring partners for Bogey, and fights with local club boxers. Although due to his extensive leg injuries he would never again achieve the fast, dancing footwork of his youth, Bogey gained a new maturity under Archie's tutelage, and learned to compensate for his slower lower body movement with faster and better punching combinations. He always fought wearing long pants or with his legs wrapped so that spectators would not be shocked by the scarring. As he regained increased muscle mass and strength, Bogey went from the middleweight class to light heavyweight, and because all fighters needed a catchy ring name, his became, naturally, Bogey "The Cowboy" Lambert.

Undefeated in his club bouts, The Cowboy began to gain a bit of a local reputation, and it wasn't long before Archie had registered him with the Scottish boxing association, and Bogey officially turned pro. However, as he had learned, the Scots were a hearty race of men and the boxers he fought now were considerably tougher competition than the over-the-hill circus pugilists he had faced back home as a boy. Still, Archie had been in the business for a long time, and he knew how to bring a young boxer along, starting him slowly, matching him against less experienced fighters, allowing him to build confidence before moving him to the next level. In addition, Bogey fought now with a new intensity, an anger he didn't fully understand for it was not a part of his fundamental character; all he knew for sure was that he needed to take his aggressions out on his opponents in the ring, or they would implode within him.

For over three years, Bogey competed all around Scotland—Edinburgh, Glasgow, Aberdeen, and in the smaller venues of Leith, Hamilton, Dunbarton, Airdries, Dunfries, Dumbarton. He fought primarily in the light heavyweight division, where he was ranked as high as #3 in the country, but he also had bouts above his class from time to time against heavyweights. However, in the course of long fights, Bogey's damaged legs would abandon him and unless he was able to knock out his opponent early, he rarely won a contest that went into the later rounds. Of course, it was not long before the other boxers and their trainers on the pro circuit learned his weakness and began to take full advantage of it, extending fights as long as they could to wear him down. As a result, Bogey "The Cowboy" Lambert was never given a shot at a title bout. Still, he saved up a good deal of prize money during those years.

In the fall of 1924, a tenacious pub fighter from Glasgow named Boy Tweedley, who had a reputation for punching below the belt, punished Bogey brutally with heavy body shots for the full 15 rounds. In his corner at the end of the fight, as they were waiting for the judges' decision while Archie unlaced his gloves, Bogey said: "I'm done, Arch, that's it, that's my last fight. As of tonight, I'm retiring."

He lost the decision and peed blood for two weeks, and two weeks after that, traveling under a false British passport obtained by one of Archie Munro's underworld connections, Bogey took the ferry across the channel, and stepped onto French soil for the first time in five years.

5

As it is for many veterans who return to the scene of a war in which they have fought, Bogey's first act upon landing in France was to make a kind of pilgrimage to the place where he and Crazy Horse had been blown up. He had not lost his fine sense of direction, and had no trouble locating the road to Mons upon which they had traveled on that long ago day. He was shocked to see that after four years much of the ruined earth had barely begun to recover, and was nearly as bleak and without flora as it had been on that distant morning. Gone at least was the barbed wire, and most of the trenches had been plowed over by optimistic farmers, hoping each year that their seeds might once again sprout in the poisoned soil. This was dangerous work, and the farmers had learned to outfit their tractors with sturdy metal plates beneath the seats, for they still periodically unearthed unexploded shells and live mines, and many still died in this way. Thus, every year for decades yet to come, the Great War would continue to claim new victims.

In a kind of patchwork fashion, certain other pieces of ground had been spared or at least had been less heavily bombed, and Bogey was heartened to see that in some meadows grass grew, golden green now in the fall, with horses and cows grazing upon it.

Through this landscape, Bogey walked and hitchhiked, accepting a ride on the last stretch in the back of a hay wagon bearing a load of fresh cut grass, the smell of which made him homesick. Although he could not expect to find the exact spot where the explosion occurred, when he felt instinctively that it was close, he jumped off the wagon. The farmer reined his team of horses up and asked Bogey if he had been a soldier, for other men had come this way on similar missions. Bogey said that, yes, he had.

"My two sons were soldiers," said the farmer, "but they did not survive the war."

"I'm very sorry for you, sir."

The farmer pointed to a farmhouse on a distant hill. "Our farm was greatly damaged," he said. "Occupied first by the *Boches*, then by the French, and then by the Americans and the British. It was partially bombed and gutted and looted. But somehow the bones of the house itself survived, and when my wife and I came back, we rebuilt. I am the third generation to farm this land, and my sons would have been the fourth, but now I am the last. If it were not for you Americans, we would all be speaking German now. I would like to invite you to come to our house for dinner, we would be honored to receive you. And if you wish, you may spend the night in our sons' room. My wife has kept it made up for the boys' return, and it would please us very much to have you sleep there."

"Thank you, sir, I would be honored to accept your invitation," Bogey answered. "May I ask you a question, sir? Did you ever hear of a man on horseback being blown up on this road on the last day of the war?"

"Many men on horseback died on this road during the war, and many men on foot," he said. "He was a relative of yours' this man, or a friend?"

"Yes."

"My name is Lefebvre," the farmer said, nodding. "We will expect you for dinner." And then he slapped the reins on the rumps of his team of horses and drove on.

Bogey walked the road, trying to remember the physical details of the landscape that morning, trying to return to the moment when the crow flew overhead and his world exploded. He had the sense that if only he could return to that exact spot, that exact moment, he might be given another chance. This time, he could ride a wide berth around the bomb, and he and Crazy Horse could continue on toward Mons, and all that had happened that day, and in the nearly five years since, would be erased, replaced by a different reality in which both he and Crazy Horse survived the war, alive and intact. And he would no longer be just the ghost of that man returning to this place.

Bogey walked on and on, but he could not find the spot.

It took him over an hour to reach the farmhouse, and his legs ached from the long day of walking. The farmer Lefebvre, and his wife, welcomed him and offered him a seat at the kitchen table and a glass of local juniper brandy. A fire burned in the hearth, and Madame Lefebvre grilled andouillette sausage upon it, and steamed cauliflower in a pot. And with the meal they drank the rich dark beer of the region and ate freshly baked bread, and afterwards she served an endive salad followed by cheeses and more brandy, and a tart made of autumn blackberries.

"That was delicious, madam," Bogey said as they sat by the fire after dinner sipping brandy and smoking.

"I've been in Scotland for a long time and they don't eat like this over there, I can tell you. Thank you." Bogey had the sense that this was the meal the woman had intended to serve her sons upon their return from the war, and now, finally, five years later, she was able to serve it to him. He was comfortable with this fine, sad couple who reminded him of the stoic, hospitable country people back home, who kept their own counsel and never complained. The farmer stood and walked from the kitchen, and in a little while he came back with a wooden wine crate.

"You asked me this afternoon about a man on horseback being blown up on the road the last day of the war," the farmer said. "We were not here then, we had been forced to abandoned the farm, and had not yet returned. But after we came back, I found many, many items from the war on my land, and I am still finding them. I have kept a small collection of these things. I do not know why I keep them…as a remembrance I suppose…in honor of the men to whom they once belonged, and perhaps in the hopes that someone might come back to claim them one day. I have in this box several items of equestrian tack, which are clearly not of French manufacture. Who knows, perhaps something may have belonged to the friend or the relative you seek here. You may look through this if you like."

When the farmer handed him the box, the very first item that Bogey pulled from it was the steel bit from Crazy Horse's bridle, with several pieces of frayed leather still attached. There was no mistaking it, for Bogey had warmed this bit in his hands thousands of times on cold mornings, before slipping it into Crazy Horse's mouth. Next he picked up one of his own spurs, in oddly good condition, the leather fastening straps cracked but intact. And then the saddle horn, which had completely detached from the saddle itself. At the bottom of the box he found one of his saddlebags, inside it the medal he had won in a bronc riding event at Cheyenne Frontier Days rodeo, and an eagle feather he had always carried for good luck. And finally, from the box he pulled his grandfather's Colt .45 Peacemaker, the barrel bent, and the cylinder frozen shut with rust.

The Lefebvres watched Bogey carefully as he examined these items, and they knew from his reaction that they surely belonged to him, and that it was he and his horse who had been blown up that day. But as is so often the case with country folk, in no matter what land, they were too discreet to ever consider asking Bogey questions, and when they saw tears welling up in his eyes, they stood and busied themselves clearing plates and cleaning the kitchen. They knew that the young man did not wish to speak of these matters, in the same way they kept their own sorrows to themselves.

"Could you take me tomorrow to the place where you found these things?" Bogey finally asked the farmer Lefebvre.

"Of course."

Bogey spent several weeks living with those good people, sleeping in their sons' room, which had been perfectly made up for them, as though they had just left and might return at any time. During the day, Bogey worked on the property with the farmer. It was work he knew and loved, and he was happy to touch the earth again. At noon and in the evening Madame Lefebvre made hearty meals for them. The couple was grateful to have the young American in their home, but then, finally, all of them knew when it was time for him to leave, for all began to feel the presence of ghosts in the house, of which Bogey was still one.

CHRYSIS

1925 – 1926

1

Despite having grown up under an authoritative father, as an only child Gabrielle had been indulged by her parents, and as a consequence it took her some time to adapt to life in Le Foyer des Jeunes Filles, the residence hall for young women. The foyer was managed by a nun, Sister Thérèse, a tiny, birdlike woman in stature, yet one who carried the implacable authority, and the all-seeing eyes of God Himself. The little sister enforced strict rules for correct comportment, proper attire, and an immutable schedule of meals, prayer, and curfew, when all residents must be in their rooms with lights out. Gabrielle knew that her parents had chosen this lodging as a means of counterbalancing both her own independent nature, as well as the bohemian influences of Montparnasse.

It was a vibrant time in the neighborhood with the grand immigration of poets, novelists, painters, sculptors, musicians, dancers—not only from France, but from all over the world—and the liberated, energized atmosphere seemed to Gabrielle the perfect antidote to life in the foyer, and to the days spent under the regulations of Professor Humbert. Indeed, male models at the atelier were not even allowed to pose there for the women unless their genitals were covered, although this was not required in the men's atelier, nor for the women models.

"But how are we to learn true human anatomy if such things are denied us?" Gabrielle asked Professor Humbert during class one day, when the male model undressed and took his pose wearing his underwear.

"Go to the Louvre, young lady," Professor Humbert suggested, "or the library to look at photographs of Michelangelo's David."

"But those are two-dimensional, representational images," she argued, "not true anatomical models. I have never seen a man's real penis before. How can I paint what I do not know?"

This remark elicited varied gasps and titters from some of the other students.

The professor cleared his throat. "You see, Mademoiselle Jungbluth," he said, "you have no need to paint it—for the simple reason that we are not painting genitalia this morning, we are painting the figure of a man."

"Is the man a eunuch, then, Professor?" Gabrielle asked.

Professor Humbert's face reddened and the students all prepared themselves for one of his legendary tantrums, each of them grateful that it was not she who was to be the recipient of his wrath. But this time the professor managed to control himself; he smiled evenly and said: "Continue your work, please, young lady."

As a small act of defiance, Gabrielle painted the model without his shorts on, but with no genitalia at all, like the figure of one of the dolls with which she once played as a child, and which even then annoyed her with their incomplete anatomies.

As the professor was making the rounds of the various easels to instruct and correct his students, he paused at Gabrielle's. "*Hmmmm,*" he said with a small, ironic smile, "not bad mademoiselle, not bad at all."

Montparnasse, only a few short blocks away, offered a view of a different world altogether, and between the time class ended at the atelier, and the early dinner hour at the foyer, Gabrielle tried to circulate as much as possible in the neighborhood. When she came out of the metro into the Carrefour Vavin, she felt briefly released from the two worlds of rules in which she spent so much of her time. If she hurried there, or the professor dismissed class early, she was just able to catch the beginning of the evening aperitif hour, before rushing back to the foyer, for if one was so much as a single minute late sitting down at table, Sister Thérèse imposed odious penalties—washing all the dinner dishes, for instance, or worse, cleaning the shared toilets on each floor, a duty one particularly did not wish to perform immediately after dinner.

But here in the "village," as the gas lights came on and the cafés filled, Gabrielle breathed an intoxicating musk of freedom, independence, and anarchy—a vibrant mélange of men and women, art and sex, love and violence, poverty and riches; it was all there, all the untidy aspects of human nature and behavior, unleashed and waiting to unfold. She knew instinctively that this was only a glimpse of what she wished to paint, these early hours of the evening when liberated, beautiful, eccentric people came out to socialize, and that beneath this, much later at night and on into the morning, lay the true stories that would captivate her imagination. She knew as well, that she did not yet possess the necessary knowledge or artistic skills to capture on canvas such richness, such complexity and contradictions.

She needed somehow to enter this seductive, unknown world herself in order to truly understand it, and this idea both excited and frightened her.

2

The Paris winter faded gradually, the clouds, cold and damp giving way finally to a tentative sunlight, the tulips blossoming in the Luxembourg gardens, the buds on the chestnut and plane trees bursting open as if in a single day, the pure unsullied bright green of first spring, the collective mood of the city immensely heartened by the simple warmth of the sun.

Gabrielle had settled into her routine at the atelier, still with a partially adversarial relationship with Professor Humbert, but one based on a certain mutual respect. They each seemed to recognize and accommodate the other's vast difference in age and point of view, an enormous generational chasm that in some cases could simply not be spanned. But they also shared a reverence for art, and for that reason, the professor allowed Gabrielle a certain latitude he might not have granted other students.

The atelier was in session through the end of July, and at the beginning of the summer, the professor chose those works he deemed worthy of display in the school's annual end-of-the-year exhibition. As a new student, who had just come in for the second semester, Gabrielle was not surprised that none of her drawings or paintings were chosen, but she could not say that she wasn't disappointed. She was a competitive girl, and believed that some of her work was superior to that of the older, more experienced women in the class. Indeed, on several occasions the professor had singled out certain of her pieces as the best of particular assignments, but all these he passed over in his final selection. Gabrielle wondered if their sometimes contentious relationship was partially responsible for this. But, in fact, Humbert himself had a different reason for withholding such awards, and that was simply to motivate the young painter toward ever better work.

As usual, the Jungbluths spent the month of August in Dieppe. Gabrielle took her easel and painting supplies with her, for Professor Humbert expected all of his students to continue working outside, *en plein air,* during their vacations and to show him the results of their efforts when the atelier resumed in the fall.

In Dieppe, the Jungbluth family took the same vacation house every summer, and this season as during the last, boys began to call on Gabrielle. Her parents allowed her to go out walking with them, or to the cinema, the theatre or musical performances in the village, but only after an interview with the colonel, the very idea of which so intimidated many potential suitors that they never actually asked her out.

Gabrielle was still a virgin, but there was one boy that summer, Roger, whom she rather liked, and one night on the beach she kissed him and let him fondle her breasts beneath her blouse. When she came home that evening the colonel noticed the gray shell fragments of the Dieppe sand still stuck to the back of his daughter's bare arms. He questioned her about this, and she said they had simply been lying on the beach, talking after the theatre. The next day the colonel went to the boy's house and spoke to his father, and that was the last time Roger came calling.

For her transgression, her father confined Gabrielle to the house for a week, and the following evening she found herself alone at home while her parents were out at a dinner engagement. Because her mother was socially inclined, during their vacation the colonel sometimes felt obligated to satisfy his wife's desire to mingle with the chic summer people in the village. Bored and with nothing to do, Gabrielle wandered into her father's study to look for a book to read. Hidden out of sight behind other books on one shelf of the bookcase, she came across a novel entitled *Aphrodite,* by a writer named Pierre Louÿs. Naturally intrigued by the provocative title and the fact that the book was secreted away in this manner, she assumed that it was a forbidden volume which must have belonged to a former guest of the house, or perhaps to the proprietors themselves. However, when she opened the cover, she was surprised to find that the title page was embossed with her father's own personal seal. Gabrielle sat down in the leather club chair and began to read.

A bit over two hours later, she turned the last page, closed the book in her lap, and breathed deeply. An erotic novel, set in ancient Alexandria, *Aphrodite* told the tragic love story of a beautiful courtesan named Chrysis and a famous sculptor, Démétrios. A strange thing had happened to Gabrielle during the reading, she felt as if she had become a character in the tale herself, as if the troubled spirit of the young courtesan had entered her own body. And now, as if coming slowly out of a kind of trance, she became conscious of the fact that she was touching herself between her legs, and she felt no shame in the act, only pleasure and comfort.

It occurred to Gabrielle in that moment that she had been living her life as two separate people, and that she had always owned the ability to suppress her true nature, to control her secret desires. She was, on the one hand, a well-brought up young lady, the dutiful daughter of an upper class military family, an attentive student in the atelier of a renowned classical painter. On the other, she was a strong, willful girl, with a mind of her own, an artistic spirit who secretly resented her privileged upbringing, the pretentions and conventions of her social class, and the standards of a male-dominated society that kept women so thoroughly subjugated. She had long since recognized that even as a little girl she had always harbored an inchoate hunger to experience another deeper, more mysterious side of life that until tonight she barely knew existed, except in the forbidden night dreams of her imagination. Only then, in the ever increasing awareness of her own erotic yearnings, were her secret fantasies sometimes allowed to come out to frolic uninhibited in the darkness. Now having read this strange, disturbing novel, which revealed dark truths about love, madness, sensuality, and art, Gabrielle felt whole and free for the first time in her life, as if her two contradictory personas had finally merged into one, and her path as an artist lay clearly before her.

On that evening, Gabrielle was reborn as Chrysis, and as a constant affirmation of her liberation she took for herself that name. For the rest of her long life she would sign all her work, *Chrysis Jungbluth*, even her work at the atelier, to the initial disapproval of Professor Humbert, who was well aware of the provenance of the name. Published in Paris in 1896, *Aphrodite,* had created quite a public controversy in the country, and had sold over 350,000 copies—the bestselling work by any living French writer at the time. Indeed, it was one of those books that everyone owned, but none admitted owning, and like Colonel Jungbluth and so many other members of respectable society, male and female, the professor himself kept a copy of the forbidden novel tucked away out of his wife's sight in the back of his own bookcase.

3

At his daughter's urging, and despite his own preference for life in the country, Colonel Jungbluth leased an apartment in Montparnasse for the family that fall. Desperate to escape the constraints of the Foyer des Jeunes Filles, Chrysis herself had found the apartment for them at 14 boulevard Edgar Quinet, across the street from the Montparnasse cemetery. The building contained a number of artists' studios, and the colonel, understanding that his daughter needed a space of her own to work independent of Humbert's atelier, also leased one of these. Chrysis was thrilled. No matter how strict her father or how structured life in his household, the colonel was no match for Sister Thérèse. In addition, Chrysis knew how to charm and manipulate her father, against which tactics the little sister had proven to be utterly impervious.

Chrysis returned alone to Paris in the early fall, two weeks before classes resumed at the atelier. Her mother, whose health was fragile, had fallen ill and the colonel was unwilling to leave his wife alone in Rouen in order to accompany his daughter. Although worried for her mother, Chrysis was secretly pleased at this rare opportunity for freedom, and to be allowed to move into the family's new apartment on her own, and into her very first studio. This latter was a fine space, on the ground floor, small but with large windows and good light, and opening up onto a treed courtyard.

Chrysis had announced to her parents that she was determined to become self-sufficient as an artist, to pay her own rent for the atelier, and she began prowling the cafés, bars and restaurants of the neighborhood trying to talk the proprietors and managers into displaying her work. However, given the sheer number of artists in the village these days, there was a great deal of competition for limited wall space.

During these few weeks alone in the city, and for the first time in her life, Chrysis was as free as everyone else she had so envied in Montparnasse during her first year here—free to dress as she wished, to wander the *quartier* at any hour, to go to the nightclubs, to drink and dance until dawn if she so chose. She felt finally like an adult, and she immersed herself completely in the life of the village.

One raucous evening in La Rotonde, she watched as a fistfight erupted between two arguing poets, one a Dadaist, the other a Surrealist. This quickly degenerated into a general melee as their respective supporters joined in, breaking dishes and chairs over each other's heads. The police finally arrived to break up the brawl and to take the perpetrators to jail for the night. In the midst of it all, at a quiet corner table, two girls dressed in men's suits and neckties kissed and nuzzled, while at a table beside them one of the surrealists poets involved in the fracas, had removed himself from the violence just in time to avoid being arrested, in order to recite erotic love poems to a popular singer of whom he was clearly enamored.

Chrysis loved all of it. With the pure objectivity of the artist/observer, she embraced this crazed human expression of spontaneous passion, of pushing the limits of convention, in which women, too, were full and equal participants. Even more than that, it was the women who seemed to generate much of the extraordinary energy that pulsated through the *quartier.* They dressed in a new style of their own, and sometimes outlandishly, they exposed their breasts, they flirted, they talked back, and they made up their own rules, thus defying the presumed authority of men. And for all this they were clearly adored, celebrated more than ever, which was a valuable lesson for young Chrysis to learn.

That fall she took to smoking Craven "A" cigarettes which were made in London and came in stylish red tin boxes, and she started indulging her own very distinctive sense of style. She went shopping for clothing in the ethnic neighborhoods of the city—at the African, Middle Eastern, and Asian markets—locales to which her mother would never take her.

With some variations, Chrysis's primary outfit for wandering the neighborhood, sketching, or painting in her atelier were Turkish pantaloons in faded jade and purple stripes, tied at the ankles with silk ties, over which she wore a maroon chenille knitted loose top with three-quarter length sleeves. Atop that she wore a putty-colored smocked farmer's coat, which she had purchased off the farmer himself during the Saturday market at Les Halles, in return for a drawing she made of the man's young son and daughter sitting on the back of the family market truck. This coat she wore open, practical for its large pockets into which she stuffed her rags, small brushes and pencils. Finally, on the top and bottom of this eclectic outfit, she wore her thick black hair loosely tied up with a long silk scarf from Indonesia, and on her feet Moroccan leather slippers.

The weekend before Chrysis started classes again at the atelier, her parents came to Paris, and she met them at the Montparnasse station. Her father looked her up and down, recognizing as he did so that his fears were being realized, that he was losing his little girl to the bohemian madness of the neighborhood.

"Your mother will take you shopping," the colonel said, "and buy you some proper clothes for the fall."

"It is lovely to see you, too, father," she said, kissing him on both cheeks.

"I think you look quite well, my dear," said her mother, who secretly envied and admired her daughter's independent artistic nature, her ability to stand up to the colonel.

As to the new first name Chrysis had assumed, and now insisted everyone call her, Colonel Jungbluth, knowing full well its origins and how she had come upon it, could hardly object too strongly. For obvious reasons, he did not wish to implicate himself in the matter with his wife, and thus he and his daughter, although they would never broach the subject, kept to themselves the secret of the novel *Aphrodite* and the courtesan Chrysis. Yet from that point forward, and for the rest of his life, the colonel would never once address his daughter by this name.

4

Classes resumed at the Atelier Humbert, and when Chrysis wasn't working there, she painted in her own atelier. She was studious and committed to her art, but on weekends, when her parents frequently returned to their house in Rouen, she took the opportunity to continue her exploration of the Montparnasse nightlife. At first, she had kept very much to the periphery, making the rounds of the clubs and cafés that were still proliferating throughout the *quartier*, getting a sense for the individual character and quirks of each establishment, learning who and what clientele might be found where. She almost always carried her sketchpad, which provided somewhat of a buffer against unwanted advances, in the same way that the privacy of writers was usually respected if they were working in their notebooks.

Chrysis was younger than the established artists of the neighborhood, but as she became a more familiar presence, inevitably she began to make friends and acquaintances. She met the artist, Jules Pascin, who like her, frequently sketched in the cafés, and was often in the company of one or more of his models. She regularly encountered the American photographer, Man Ray in Le Dôme or La Rotonde; he was almost always with the woman everyone called simply Kiki, the favorite artists' model of the neighborhood, who was striking, gay and stylish, who wore homemade outfits that often showed her breasts, and who clearly had a mind of her own. Sometimes Kiki came to the café wrapped in a fur coat, which if it happened to fall open at the table, revealed that she was entirely naked underneath. This she explained as a practical matter: she had an appointment to pose, and did not wish to have elastic underwear marks visible on her skin.

One day in Le Dôme, Chrysis met the funny little Japanese artist Foujita, with his bangs, tiny moustache, and round horn-rimmed glasses. He asked her to come to his studio on the nearby rue Delambre to pose for him, but she declined, as she always did this invitation. Chrysis was familiar with Foujita's work, having seen it at exhibitions at the Salon d'Automne. He was quite famous in the Paris art world, and in April of that year had been awarded the *Légion d'Honneur.* Privately, she wondered how much of his success was due to Foujita's eccentricity and exoticism, for she believed that he was a far better self-promoter than he was a painter.

Chrysis often saw Picasso on the streets or in one or another of the cafés. He was clearly the most famous of the artists in the neighborhood, and she was always too shy to speak to him. But one day when she spotted Georges Braque in La Rotonde, she approached him and introduced herself as a student of his former teacher, Professor Jacques Ferdnand Humbert.

"That old man is still at it then, is he?" Braque said. "I imagine he is more irascible than ever. You know I studied under him over 20 years ago. He is a fine teacher, and I learned a great deal from him. However we have lost touch over the years. He tolerated my Fauve work, but I'm afraid he never forgave me for Cubism."

"Yes, sir, I know," Chrysis said. "He still talks about you in class. But despite his disdain for Cubism, he holds you in very high esteem."

"That is fine to know, young lady," Braque said, "thank you. Good luck to you. And please give the professor my best regards."

Chrysis became friendly with the Russian artist Chaim Soutine, who some years earlier had also studied in one of the ateliers at L'École des Beaux-Arts. Soutine seemed a gentle, simple man, and Chrysis admired his proletariat work clothes, which he often wore to the cafés. One day he invited her to come back with him to see some of his work at his studio on the rue Saint Gothard. The painter was working at the time on a series of studies inspired by Rembrandt's *Beef Carcass,* and Chrysis was astonished to see that he had a whole butchered cow hanging in his studio, which moreover, was beginning to rot, the stench of which made her feel faint. "You see, young lady," said Soutine, as he showed her the canvas in progress on his easel, "this is the potential power of art: it can triumph over putridity, even be inspired by it. Remember this, if something truly engages you, obsesses you, there is no subject off limits to the artist."

On another day in Le Dôme, Chrysis met the Polish artist Moïse Kisling, who in turn introduced her to one of his younger countryman, a gypsy poet named Casmir Luka, who had only recently arrived in Paris. He was a large, handsome young man, dark-skinned with curly black hair, a square jaw and high cheekbones. Chrysis was attracted to the gypsy and asked if she could sketch him. "Yes, you may sketch me, if I may write a poem about you," he said. "And also if you buy me a bowl of soup. For I am very poor."

In addition to the popular gathering places clustered around the Carrefour Vavin, Chrysis began to frequent some of the smaller, more intimate night spots, especially those offering music and dancing, such as Le Jockey, La Cignone, Le Parnasse, La Jungle, and especially Le Bal Nègre, a tiny, out-of-the-way club on the rue Blomet, where immigrant workers from the Antilles gathered, and Negro jazz bands played at night. She loved to dance, loved jazz and blues music, and she learned all the new steps being brought to Paris by the massive post-war influx of Americans. She loved the black musicians, and at the clubs she danced with both men and women, whoever asked her first, she did not care, the point was simply to dance, to keep moving, to expend her boundless energy. It sometimes happened that when a woman held her, their bodies brushing casually against each other to the sensuous rhythm of the music, Chrysis felt certain stirrings previously unknown to her. This did not disturb her, nor did she try to suppress these sensations; quite the contrary, she was intrigued by the fact that yet another unknown yearning was revealing itself to her. She was young, alive, receptive to all stimuli, she made no distinction between art and life, she hungered for all of it.

Chrysis sometimes crossed over to the right bank to patronize Le Boeuf sur le Toit (The Cow on the Roof), which had the largest dance floor and some of the best jazz in the city. There she often saw the celebrated playwright, Jean Cocteau, holding court, and the woman Kiki singing at the piano; she had a ghastly voice, but a lively, infectious talking/singing style, and usually half-drunk, she performed bawdy songs that charmed and titillated the audience. The bar was decorated with paintings by

Francis Picabia, whose early Dada, and later Surrealist work was not a style Chrysis found particularly interesting. But then she had not been to war and was not yet old enough or sufficiently experienced to have become a cynic or a deconstructionist. The world still seemed to her a grand place, full of adventure, boundless promise and hope, full of color, sensuality, light and laughter, and those were the things she wished to capture in her paintings.

Besides the older established artists, the village in those years was filled with dozens, hundreds, thousands of younger aspiring novelists, poets, painters, sculptors, models, students, and sundry hangers-on, of all races and nationalities, the vast majority of whom would never be known in their respective fields, nor ever heard from again. But in that brief grace moment of youth, none could know this yet, and to those like Chrysis who were actually working at their crafts, everything seemed still possible, their dreams not yet overwhelmed by the lonely march of time and reality.

5

In the fall of that year, a new café, Le Select, opened on the boulevard Montparnasse. It became immediately popular with the writers and painters of the village, many of whom abandoned La Rotonde and Le Dôme, which were being increasingly overrun with tourists, to make this their favorite new meeting place.

One cold, damp late afternoon in mid-November, the streets strewn with soggy brown leaves and a light snow falling, Chrysis approached Le Select. Feeling a bit of autumnal melancholy, she peered through the partially fogged window, rivulets of condensation running down the glass from the warmth inside. It was the sort of day in which having some company seemed a welcome idea, and she looked to see if any of her friends or acquaintances might be inside.

She saw a man sitting alone at a table against the wall, writing in a notebook, and in that exact instant he looked up and their eyes met, he from inside the warm café, she outside on the cold sidewalk. He was clearly focused on whatever he was writing for although he looked directly in her eyes, his gaze seemed to pass right through her, as if she was invisible or transparent. Yet in that momentary flashing glance, Chrysis thought that she had fallen in love. She had never before seen such extraordinary eyes—dark, kind, sad, haunted eyes, that caused her breath to catch in her throat, and gave her a strange sensation of falling. She flushed and looked away, went to the door and entered, removing her scarf and coat beneath which she carried her sketchpad against the snow falling outside. She hung her coat on the rack by the door, chose a table across the room from the man, opened her pad and discreetly began to draw him.

Every now and then the man would pause in his writing and look up thoughtfully, as if considering a word or a turn of phrase, and then he would return to his work. He seemed in some strange way to be completely self-contained, as if he existed entirely within himself, somehow not quite connected to the external world, only his eyes in those brief moments betraying some secret pain. Chrysis thought that if only she could capture the subtle emotion expressed in those eyes, then she would be a true artist.

The man had dark hair and strong features, and even seated it was clear that he was a tall and rangy. As Chrysis sketched, she noticed, too, that he had beautifully formed hands—the hands of a man who did physical labor—and as she studied and outlined them on her pad, she became aroused as she imagined those hands caressing her body.

When she was finishing her drawing, Chrysis looked again at the man's face as he wrote, and she thought she saw tears appear in the corner of his eyes. She looked quickly away, feeling that she had intruded upon some intensely private moment. She finished her drawing and set her sketchbook down on the table, and at nearly the same moment the man closed his notebook. He reached into his pocket, pulled out change, looked at the bill, and dropped a few coins on the saucer. He stood. She saw that he was wearing cowboy boots and Levis. Cowboys and Indians were all the rage these days in Montparnasse, particularly at the balls when everyone dressed up in costume and pretended to be someone or something else. But she did not think that this outfit was an affectation on the man's part, or that he was pretending.

As he was walking toward the coat rack by the door, he passed her table without looking at her, and Chrysis said: "Excuse me, sir, but I made a drawing of you. Would you like to see it?"

The man stopped, turned, and regarded her directly with those arresting eyes, as if seeing her for the first time, as if he hadn't quite understood what she had said to him, or as if he was puzzled at having been thus addressed. Chrysis felt herself blushing. "I'm very sorry to disturb you, sir," she said, nonplussed by the strange puissance of his gaze, which seemed to possess a kind of omniscience, as if he was looking out of his wounded soul directly into hers. In that instant, she lost her confidence, and felt like a silly, stammering schoolgirl. "I just...I just thought you might like to see the sketch I made of you while you were working. May I...may I show it to you?"

The man continued to stare at her, his dark eyes seeming to lay open her chest, exposing her beating heart, all her secret fears and desires spilling out on the floor of the café in a pool of blood. Finally, he shook his head. "*Non, non merci,*" he said, and he walked to the door, took a long canvas coat from the rack, slipped it on, pulled the collar high around his neck, removed a cowboy hat from the rack, settled it on his head, and without looking back pushed out the door and disappeared into the darkening winter evening.

Chrysis watched him go, her heart racing, her body flushed and her skin tingling, a sensation that felt like the prelude to an orgasm. Only later did it finally occur to her that she did not even know the man's name, or if she would ever see him again.

6

Chrysis left Le Select and walked down the street to Le Dôme, where she knew she would find her friend, Casmir, the young gypsy poet to whom Kisling had introduced her. In his state of poverty, Casmir wore self-mended clothes and worn shoes and each time she saw him he looked a little shabbier. He wrote short poems on cocktail napkins and tried to sell them to the tourists, who sometimes took pity upon him. Chrysis did not know whether or not he was a good poet, but he seemed a kind, gentle man, and she worried about how he would survive in Paris.

"May I sit with you, Casmir?" she asked.

"Of course, Chrysis," he answered. "Will you buy me a bowl of soup?"

"Yes, whatever you want. I came looking for you because I want to ask you a personal favor."

"Very well, ask me."

"I think I've fallen in love."

"When?"

"Just now."

"With me?"

"No, not with you," Chrysis said with a soft smile. "But I want you to take me home with you. After you eat your soup, I want you to take me home and teach me about love."

It was less than a five-minute walk from Le Dôme to the poet's apartment, a cold water garret around the corner on the rue de Chevreuse. They walked quickly and did not speak. They climbed the dim staircase to the top floor, and Casmir let them in with his key. "It is not much," he said, apologetically, "but I do not have money."

Indeed, it wasn't much, but Chrysis didn't care.

"Sit down, please," he said, indicating a frail wooden chair at his small kitchen table, which was covered with cocktail napkins and other scraps of paper on which were written poems or fragments of poems. Chrysis kept her coat on for it was cold in the flat.

Casmir put paper and sticks of wood in a cast iron stove and lit it with a match. "Firewood is very expensive, isn't it?" he said. "Kisling gave me some of his."

"Do you write all your poems in Polish, or do you also write in French?" Chrysis asked.

"Yes, I am learning to write in French," he said, "because I hope to be published here and I do not trust a translator to correctly interpret my poems. And I am also learning to write in English because the American tourists have the most money."

"Do you ever write poems about love?" she asked.

"All of my poems are about love. That and death are the only worthy subjects for a true poet."

"Will you read one of them to me?"

Casmir ran his hand through the napkins and paper scraps on the kitchen table, until finally picking a piece up. "Here it is," he said. "I shall read you the poem I wrote while you were sketching me. It is very short. He cleared his throat. The title of this poem is: '*The Girl Painter Who Wants Me.*'

"*She draws me with her eyes*
they speak as well as see

And now she opens her legs to me
and I kiss her there tenderly."

He looked up from his notebook and smiled expectantly at Chrysis.

"That's it?" she asked. "That's the whole poem?"

He shrugged. "Perhaps. It is all I have written so far. Is it not enough?"

"How did you know I wanted you?"

"Because I have seen that you have a great curiosity about such matters," he said, "but little experience. I am hungry for soup, you are hungry for sexual experience, you crave it. Am I not correct?" He smiled, and put his hand on her knee.

"Yes, it is true. I want to know everything, to experience all of it, to feel every sensation. Will you show me?"

Casmir knelt like a supplicant on the floor before Chrysis. He opened her farmer's coat, untied the drawstring of her pantaloons and slipped them down over her legs. He ran his hands lightly up her thighs, his fingers on the outside, his thumbs stroking the soft pale skin inside, raising gooseflesh, whether from the cold or arousal she could not tell. "You are wearing no culottes," he said.

"I took them off in the toilet at Le Dôme," Chrysis said. "I thought it would make things easier."

"How old are you?"

"Eighteen, almost nineteen. And you?"

"Twenty-four. You are a very bold girl, Chrysis, and yet this is the first time for you, is it not?"

"Yes."

"Why have you waited so long?"

"Until recently I was living with the nuns in the foyer for young women, and now I live with my parents."

"And why do you not do it first with this man with whom you are in love?"

"He does not yet know that we are in love," she said. "He does not even know that I exist. I may never see him again. But if I do, I wish to be ready to receive him correctly."

"I hope you never see him again."

"Why do you say that?"

"Because love sensed, but unrealized, is the best love of all."

"Why?"

"Because then it lives on as a dream, it never dies, is never disappointed. If you never see this man again, some small part of you will love him for the rest of your life. You will always retain the memory of a pure love. Love actualized is rarely so enduring. If you do see him again, it will end badly. It almost always does. He will leave you, or you will leave him, he will die or you will die—one or both of you will be hurt, heartbroken, devastated. That is just how love is. I wrote a poem about this once."

"That sounds like a very depressing poem."

Casmir took her gently by the hips and pulled her lower body toward him. He lowered his face to Chrysis's lap, his lips grazing the soft hairs of her slender upper thighs. She parted her legs to his tongue. "You were born by the sea," he whispered. "I can taste the sea."

"Yes."

He picked her up and carried her to the bed, a thin straw mattress covered in hemp, upon it a thick duvet of red-striped ticking filled with feathers. He laid her down atop the bed, puffs of feathers escaping pinholes in the duvet, like flocks of tiny birds.

Beneath the duvet, the bed was cold at first but then it became warm. Chrysis did not know if Casmir was much of a poet, but he was a fine, sweet lover, and he made her happy that first time, a kind of happiness she had only imagined in her fantasies. She once believed that there could be nothing more wonderful than the inner world of color and form in which she lived, the painter's world of her imagination. But she knew now that a whole new universe was opening up to her.

7

Chrysis looked everywhere for the man she had seen in Le Select. She went back again and again, always expecting to find him there, but always disappointed. She searched all the cafés and bars, she asked around the neighborhood. He had only spoken those three words to her, "*Non, non merci*," but she assumed from his accent and his attire that he was an American. She began to think that he must have been a tourist; there were more American tourists in Paris than ever before, and although the majority of them still took lodging in hotels on the Right Bank, all had by now heard of the crazy artists of Montparnasse, and they flocked there to see them, the *quartier* becoming a kind of tourist destination in its own right, something to be added to one's list of vacation "to do" items: the Louvre, Notre Dame, the Eiffel Tour, and Montparnasse—its bars, cafés, and nightclubs—where the tourists hoped to catch sight of living artists rather than look at the work of dead ones. However, among the tourists were also a number of poseurs, those who began to affect the styles and attire of the local artists so that often only the regular habitués could tell the difference between them.

And so the weeks and the months slipped by, spring came, and the first buds on the plane trees in the Luxembourg Gardens began to open. Chrysis had given up hope of ever finding the man, and she assumed that he must have gone back to America at the end of his Parisian vacation. Perhaps Casmir was right, and this was the purest love of all: unrealized. From the sketch she had made of him on that cold afternoon in November, she painted a portrait, but she could never get his eyes right, no matter how many times she repainted them, and finally, disgusted, she threw the portrait out.

Although she was not in love with him, Chrysis continued to see the gypsy poet. He introduced her to some of his friends, and he took her to her first orgy, where she experienced the hedonistic pleasures of giving oneself over to complete sensual indulgence, the liberating quest for satisfaction.

The orgy was held in the basement of a private club, by invitation only, and only couples had been invited. On descending the staircase into the dim, candlelit room, Chrysis felt her heart beating, a warm flush of excitement washing over her face. She had no idea what to expect and Casmir had answered none of her questions. He would only say: "The entire point is to discover the unknown, to discover yourself, to seek the deep mysteries of your own erotic nature. Each time is different and I could not describe it to you if I wanted to. And if I could, there would be nothing left for you to discover. You may do anything you wish to do, except to hurt another, or you may do nothing at all if you so choose. There will be a woman there, a kind of *directrice,* to help you."

The basement was so dimly lit that it took some time for Chrysis's eyes to adjust, and even then, all she could make out was the vague outline of human forms locked in various acts. She would have had to approach closer even to identify the men from the women. There was a primal odor in the air, the pungent musk of human fertility, an earthy hormonal mixture of male and female secretions, the scent of lust.

An older woman approached. She was elegantly dressed, slightly stout and heavy-breasted, but Chrysis could see that she had once been very beautiful, and was still beautiful. Suddenly, Casmir seemed to have vanished into the darkness. The woman took Chrysis's coat. "You are new here," she said. "Our rules are simple. We use only fictional names. We do not ask personal questions. We are, to each other, simply bodies, skin and flesh, hands and mouths, organs and orifices. You may sit at one of the tables, have a glass of champagne, and wait for someone to come to you. But if he or she, or they, do not please you, you are under no obligation to join them. Indeed, you are under no obligation to participate at all if you so choose. If you wish I can also direct you to a party. Tell me, then, my dear, what do you seek here? What are your preferences?

"I have no preferences," Chrysis said, "I have not yet had time to form them. I seek experience. I seek knowledge. I seek everything."

"Excellent. Then I know just the party to initiate you. But first I must wash you. It is our standard procedure."

The woman led Chrysis into a spotless white bathroom, also lit by candles. With expert, practiced hands, she began to undress her, slipping the dress over her head, removing her bra, slip and panties. Chrysis was passive, compliant. "You are lovely," said the woman, running her hand lightly up Chrysis's thigh, over the swell of her hip, to her waist, across her stomach, up over her breasts, the woman's palm just grazing her nipples, across her flushed chest, to her shoulder, gently caressing her neck, and finally cupping her cheek. This exploratory touch the woman performed much as a prospective buyer might explore the lines of a young colt in the sale ring, as if she had done it a thousand times before. "Yes, perfectly lovely, you will make a wonderful addition to our group. Your name here tonight will be Aphrodite, goddess of love. Does that suit you, my dear?"

Chrysis smiled. "Very much."

The woman drew warm water into a large copper bowl, scented with drops of lavender oil, and with a soft cloth she began to gently wash Chrysis, beginning with her feet, her legs and sex, her anus, her breasts and back. She took a white towel from a stack on the counter, dried her, and covered her with a white silk robe that draped beautifully over her body.

"There," the woman said, stepping back and looking at her with satisfaction. "You are ready now. Are you nervous?"

"A little, yes. I am excited."

"Good. As you should be."

She led Chrysis back into the main salon, where a muscular black man, wearing only a loin cloth approached with a tray upon which stood a single glass of champagne. "Drink this," said the woman, handing the glass to her, taking the tray from the black man, and cupping his cheek affectionately. "You see who I bring you, my beautiful Zeus?" she said to him. "Aphrodite." And to Chrysis she said. "You will go with Zeus to meet some of the others, and there you will experience pleasure such as you have never before known or even imagined."

Chrysis saw that the black man was looking at her, becoming aroused beneath his loin cloth, and the sight of his enlarging sex sent a tremor from deep in her loins up through her torso, and down her arms to the tips of her fingers.

Zeus took her by the arm and led her to a dark corner of the room, where by the light of candle sconces she could just make out the bodies of three other people on a bed of white sheets and pillows. Zeus untied her belted robe, slipped it over her shoulders and let it fall to the floor behind her. He untied the leather of his loin cloth and it, too, fell. He stood very close to her then, leaned down and kissed her neck lightly. Chrysis felt his sex brush her thigh. "Sit down," he whispered in her ear, and he lowered her gently to the bed.

Now by the faint flickering glow of candles, she saw two other women, one black, one white, and a white man. They smiled at her in welcome. And then she was suddenly enveloped by the specific warmth and rich scent of human bodies in sexual congress, the tactile exploration of hands and fingers, lips and tongues, men and women, the textures of skin, muscles, breasts, the gliding dampness, the pulsing heartbeat of organs. Lightheaded with desire, overwhelmed by an insatiable passion, Chrysis in a state of joy.

BOGEY

1925

1

Archie Munro had given Bogey the name of one of his old boxing cronies who lived in Paris, a retired flyweight from Liverpool named Jimmie Charters, the barman at an establishment called the Dingo American Bar and Restaurant, on the rue Delambre. It was only a short walk from the Gare Montparnasse and upon Bogey's arrival on the train he went directly there.

"I've been expecting you, mate," said Jimmie Charters, coming around from behind the bar, wiping his wet hands on his apron. He was a cherub-faced, smiling fellow. "Archie wrote me about you. He said you were a fine boxer and if not for your bad legs, you would have been a contender for the light heavyweight crown."

"I don't know about that, sir," Bogey said. "Those Scots are mighty tough customers."

"Indeed they are, mate," said Jimmie, chuckling, "indeed they are. I don't know if Archie told you or not, but at the very end of his career and the beginning of mine, I fought him in a couple of exhibitions in Glasgow. After that first bout, I felt like puking the next time I had step into the ring with him. Even past his prime he was a bulldog, that Archie; he just kept coming at you."

"Yes, sir, and he was just as tenacious as a trainer," said Bogey. "The only way I could get him off my back was to retire and move to France."

"Exactly how I escaped the bloke! Call me, Jimmie, mate, no one around here calls me sir. Now listen, I've spoken to the owner and you can work right here at the Dingo, if you'd like. You'll start in the kitchen washing dishes. How's your French?"

"I get by."

"Good, in that case, you may get a shot at waiting tables. We get more Americans and Brits in here than we do French, but you still have to be able to speak the language. You can stay at my flat until we find you a place of your own."

"Thank you, Jimmie, I sure do appreciate it," Bogey said. "I don't know what else Archie told you about me, about how I hurt my legs and all. But whatever it was, I'd be real grateful if you would keep it to yourself."

"Say no more, mate," Jimmie said, holding up his hand. "In my profession, discretion is everything." He pulled a set of keys from his pocket, handed them to Bogey, gave him directions to his flat which was right around the corner in Delambre Square, told him to leave his things off there, clean up and come back later that evening to meet the owner.

Bogey started working at the Dingo the next day. It was menial work, but he liked the sense of routine and anonymity. Except for Jimmie, no one bothered to talk much to the new dishwasher, and that was fine with him. He preferred to be left alone, to be a sort of fly on the wall, listening to the cooks and the waiters in their spirited exchanges and squabbles. From what few glimpses he caught of the actual bar and restaurant during work hours, he could see that it was a lively place.

Business was booming, and after two weeks in the kitchen, Bogey was put to work as a waiter's apprentice, clearing and setting tables, filling water glasses, and delivering food when things were busy. He was given the uniform of a white shirt, a black bowtie, a pair of black trousers, and a long white apron.

Bogey enjoyed working on the floor, overhearing snatches of conversation in various languages, conversations in which he did not need to participate, and often didn't understand in any case. As Jimmie had suggested, there were many Americans as well as British among the clientele, but even when they addressed him in English, as most did, Bogey always responded in French. He did not know exactly why, but he wanted to keep a certain distance, particularly from his own countrymen. After seven years in Europe, he noticed now how loud Americans were, and he knew that if he was identified as a fellow countrymen, he would invariably be asked questions which he had no interest in answering. He liked that the customers spoke so frankly and sometimes so intimately among themselves as he cleared their tables and filled their glasses, as if he was invisible, as if he did not exist.

Bogey thought that he had never before seen so many beautiful women as there were in Paris, and he noticed that even those who were not classically beautiful had such a sense of style and confidence that they became beautiful. He had not been with a girl in the five years since he had awakened in the war hospital, for although he had had a number of opportunities during his time in Scotland, he was ashamed of his scarred legs, and did not want anyone to see them. Still, he loved to look at the women who came through the door of the Dingo, or just walked by on the sidewalk outside, and he enjoyed listening to them as they chattered on. Sometimes the girls flirted with him, and he liked that, too.

2

Bogey had started writing stories again while he was in the hospital in Scotland, and this he had continued throughout his three-year boxing career. Now he carried his notebook in the pocket of his waiter's apron, jotting down various observations during cigarette breaks, or after work. One afternoon several weeks after he started working at the Dingo, Jimmie came upon him in the back hallway while he was making some notes. "Ah, don't tell me we have yet another writer in town!" said the barman. "You've been holding out on me, mate."

"I'm not really a writer, Jimmie, I just write things down now and then."

"Yes, that's what writers do, Bogart, in case you hadn't heard, they write things down."

"Well, what I write down reads more like a grocery list than it does like real writing," Bogey said. "Sometimes I listen to those French poets arguing at Le Dôme or La Rotonde about Dadaism and Surrealism, and even though I mostly understand what they're saying, I don't know what the hell they're talking about."

"I'm no intellectual, mate," said Jimmie, "but the fact is, I'm not so sure they know what they're talking about, either. If you'd like, I can introduce you to some of the American writers who come in here. I'm sure you've seen and heard them."

"That's alright, Jimmie. Thanks anyway, but I just write for myself. I'm not really interested in talking about it."

"Archie told me that you keep to yourself," Jimmie said. "I don't mean to pry into your personal business, Bogart, but wouldn't you like to make some friends... maybe get to know some girls? Or don't you like girls? Seems to be a lot of that going around the neighborhood these days. But Archie didn't say you were a homo."

"I'm not a homo, Jimmy," Bogey said, "I like girls just fine."

"Sure, I know you do, mate, I've watched you looking at them. I'm just having some fun with you. Speaking of which, I have a friend, one of the Americans, big boxing fan, loves to spar himself, but strictly an amateur. I want to play a little joke on him, and I need your help."

"I owe you, Jimmie, I'll do anything you ask, as long as it doesn't involve boxing. I'm retired, remember?"

"I know you are, mate," Jimmie said. "But this wouldn't be a real fight, just a few rounds of light sparring. I just want to play a little joke on my buddy, and I want you to help me.

"Ok, Jimmie, I think I'm getting the picture."

"Of course you are, mate!"

3

The following afternoon, Jimmie summoned Bogey to the bar. "Bogey, I'd like you to meet a good friend of mine," he said, and a large man turned around with an open smile. "This is Jake Barnes, he's a writer. Jake, this is our newest employee, Bogart Lambert. Bogey hails from the state of Colorado. He does some writing himself."

"Pleased to meet you, Jake," Bogey said, shaking the man's hand.

"Likewise, Bogey," said the man. "I haven't met too many westerners in Paris. What brings you here?"

"I came over for the war," Bogey said. "And just kind of stayed around."

Barnes nodded. "Served in Italy, myself. Red Cross Ambulance Service. Did you see much action, Bogey?"

"No, I was just a courier not a combatant."

"Well, you're damn lucky for that. I wasn't supposed to be a combatant either, but I still got all blown to hell. Mortar shell hit my ambulance two months after I arrived. Spent six months in hospital in Italy before they shipped me home. What kind of writing do you do?"

"Nothing much," Bogey said. "Jimmie exaggerates. I'm not really a writer."

"You look like you can take care of yourself, Bogey," Barnes said. "You ever do any boxing?"

Bogey cut a glance at Jimmie behind the bar. "I boxed a little when I was younger, Jake."

Barnes sized him up for a moment. "It's not easy for me to find sparring partners in my weight class over here," he said. "I think I've got a few pounds on you, but I'd say you're at least a light heavyweight, am I right? Jimmie, why don't you bring Bogey over to the gym one day when you're both off work? You can serve as his second. What would you say to going a few rounds with me, Bogey?"

"I'm out of shape, Jake," Bogey said. "And you look like you pack a punch. You'd have to go easy on me."

"No problem. Just a little light sparring, no one will get hurt. Isn't that right, Jimmie?"

The sparring session was arranged for a morning three days later.

"How good a fighter is this guy?" Bogey asked Jimmie on the metro ride to the gym. "Tell me about his style."

"I told you, mate, he's strictly amateur," Jimmie answered. "Doesn't have much style, very clumsy footwork. But he is strong, and you're right about one thing, he can punch. What he likes to do, especially with new opponents the first time he gets them in the ring, is he likes to sucker punch them, to hit them early and a lot harder than you usually do sparring. He likes to knock people down, give bloody noses or black eyes, and then he brags about it later at the bar. That's exactly what he'll do with you, he'll try to tag you early on with a big punch, and put you down before you've had a chance to feel each other out. But trust me, you'll see it coming in plenty of time. You could sit down and drink an *aperitif* while he's winding up for that punch, that's how much he telegraphs it."

"So what is it exactly you want me to do, Jimmie?" Bogey asked.

"I want you to wait for his money punch, which, as I say, you will have no trouble slipping, and then I want you to tag him. I don't want you to hurt him, but put him on the canvas. You know how to do that, don't you Bogey?"

"Sure, Jimmy, I know how to do that."

Barnes came to the gym with his second, an American name Harry MacElhone, the proprietor of Harry's New York Bar on the Right Bank. Jimmie and Bogey had arrived early so that they could fit Bogey with gloves, and they were already waiting in the ring when Barnes made his entrance.

Gone was his easy jocularity from the bar; all business now, Barnes came out of the locker room as if entering the arena at Madison Square Garden for a title fight, instead of a sparring session at a slightly shabby Parisian gym, bouncing on his toes and shadow boxing as he approached the ring. Bogey assessed the big man's movements and his physique in the same way his father had taught him with the circus pugilists back home, and he smiled for he could see already that Barnes lacked a certain innate athleticism. He noticed, too, that although he had thick, muscular arms, they were somewhat short, without the reach of his own.

"How you feeling today, kid?" Barnes asked. "You ready for me?"

His diminutive use of the word "kid" amused Bogey, too, for he guessed that they were roughly the same age. "I sure hope so, Jake," he answered.

The gym owner, a man named Patrice Lacas, himself a retired prizefighter, had joined them, introductions were made, and the rules determined. It was agreed that it would be an all-out sparring contest, meaning full-force punches as in a real bout, but of a duration of only three rounds. In the event of a knockdown, whether or not it was a full knockout, the fight would be called. Patrice would serve as judge, and in the event of a tie-score after the third round, additional sudden-death rounds would be added until a winner was declared.

"Jimmie, my friend, I hate to take your hard-earned cash," said Harry MacElhone, "but what would you say to a small wager?"

"I was waiting for you to ask me that, Harry," Jimmie answered. "But the truth is, I've never seen this young man fight, myself, and I understand that it has been some time since he's been in the ring. I'm willing to place a wager with you but as you have a known fighter in your corner, as well as a considerable weight advantage, I would expect favorable odds."

The two seconds then stepped away from the ring to confer privately, placed a bet and shook hands.

Patrice Lacas rang the bell. Intending to give his opponent no quarter and no time to recover whatever rusty boxing skills he might once have owned, Barnes came out of his corner like a charging bull. For his part, Bogey looked tentative, as if he might even be a little afraid of the big man bearing down on him. Barnes came in, fists high, head low, he jabbed twice with his left, feinted once with his right, jabbed twice more, powerful jabs that Bogey could feel through the thin gym gloves as he deflected them. It was true that the man was strong, and his punches possessed a certain authority. Then he could see Barnes winding up for the money punch, just like Jimmie had told him. It seemed to Bogey, as it often had when he was fighting professionally, that everything was unfolding in a kind of slow motion, as if he had all the time in the world. Barnes threw the punch, Bogey slipped it easily, feeling just the brush of the glove against his cheek. And he could see that having failed to connect, the big man had thrown himself off-balance, lurching forward and sideways. Bogey stepped in then, his left hand raised, partially obscuring his opponent's view, and with perfect economy of effort, he threw his signature right uppercut, catching Barnes under the chin, staggering him. The big man stumbled backwards, trying to keep his balance, but down he went, landing heavily on his ass. Barnes sat there on the canvas for a moment, stunned, then shook himself like a wet dog. He looked over at Jimmie in Bogey's corner, and he smiled a lopsided grin. "*Why you flyweight son-of-a-bitch, you…*"

"Jake," said Jimmie, "I'd like to introduce you to Bogart "The Cowboy" Lambert, formerly ranked #3 in Scotland in the light heavyweight division."

"*You flyweight son-of-a-bitch, you…*" Barnes repeated, shaking his head.

Bogey untied his right glove with his teeth, and pulled it off under his arm. He approached Barnes where he still sat on the canvas, and held out his hand. "Can I give you a hand up, kid?" he asked.

4

With Jimmie's help, Bogey found a tiny, inexpensive studio apartment on the rue Boissonnade, where he shared a toilet at the end of the hall with three other residents. It was full winter now, the apartment cold and damp, and on his days and nights off, Bogey had taken to spending time in some of the other neighborhood cafés and bars. These places were always warm, and he would order a coffee, a beer, a whiskey or a glass of wine depending on the time of day, and sit for hours alternately writing in his notebook, and reading books or the newspapers. Many writers in the *quartier* availed themselves thus of the cafés, and a number of painters sketched there as well, so that these convivial establishments served also as offices and studios for them.

Bogey began to meet a few people in the cafés. One day he was writing in La Rotonde when an American Indian entered. He carried an artist's sketchpad, sat down at a table next to Bogey and began to draw. When the waiter came to take his order, the Indian spoke in perfectly accented French. The waiter asked Bogey if he would like another coffee, and after Bogey responded, the Indian turned to him, and said in English: "American?"

Bogey laughed. "That obvious, is it?" he said.

"Where are you from?"

"Northern Colorado. You?"

"Eastern Montana, originally."

"Northern Cheyenne?"

"How did you know that?"

"I used to rodeo up that way," Bogey said. "I've been on your reservation. How is it that you speak such perfect French?"

"I mostly grew up here," the Cheyenne answered. "My parents were in Buffalo Bill's Wild West Show. They were trick riders. They brought me to France in 1905 when I was just a young boy. They liked it over here; they found the French less racist than the Americans, and after the tour was over, they quit the show and stayed on. Buffalo Bill Cody had been good to them and they were able to buy a little ranch in the Camargue with their savings. They raise and train Carmargue horses. It is an ancient breed, that reminded them of the wild prairie ponies of their ancestors. Now and then they still perform riding exhibitions in circuses or at rodeos and festivals."

"What's your name?"

"Jerome Running Bear."

"Pleased to meet you, Jerome. I'm Bogart Lambert, most folks call me Bogey."

And thus, besides Jimmie, Jerome Running Bear became Bogey's first friend in Paris, and sometimes when they ran into each other in one or another of the cafés, they would sit together, while Jerome sketched and Bogey wrote, two Americans, the cowboy and the Indian. Bogey learned that Jerome had studied art in Paris.

"We had fine native artists in my tribe," he told Bogey, "and they were much honored by the People. But they never learned perspective, everything was flat and two-dimensional in the manner of children's artwork. Growing up in France, of course, I was exposed to great art and I learned another way to paint."

With the natural taciturnity of his race, Jerome did not ask Bogey questions about where he had been, or why he was in Paris. But he sensed that Bogey had been a warrior, and that he was caught in some kind of limbo between two lives. This was something that American Indians understood instinctively, even those a generation or two removed from tribal life, for they themselves lived in limbo, between the world as their people once knew it, and as it became under the white man.

5

One night Bogey and Jerome were having a drink at a small working-class bar on the avenue du Maine. It was one of those anonymous drinking establishments that had neither a sign nor a name. They were standing at the end of the bar when three American sailors, already half-drunk and talking loudly, entered. The United States Government had recently sent three ships to France which were docked in Le Havre, and the *quartier* itself had been infested for days with seamen on extended shore leave.

"Well, look here, Randy," said one of the sailors, "isn't that the faggot Injun' who tried to blow you last night?"

"It's him alright," said the one called Randy, stepping up to the bar to the right of Jerome. "Offered to pay me if he could suck me off."

The other two sailors took up positions at the bar to Bogey's left.

"This your boyfriend, Chief?" asked the second sailor to the left of Bogey. "And does he know what his big bad brave was up to last night?"

Bogey turned to Jerome, and spoke in French: "Do you know how to fight?"

"No, I'm a pacifist," Jerome answered.

"Who's ever heard of a homosexual pacifist Cheyenne?" said Bogey.

"I try not to be a stereotypical redskin."

"Are you two faggots having a little lover's spat, Frenchy?" the sailor on the left of Bogey asked him. "Just because you found out your boyfriend here tried to suck sailor dick? And what's with the cowboy get-up, anyway? Is that how you perverts in France get off, playing cowboy and Indian together?"

Now Bogey turned to the sailor, and spoke in English. "Listen, kid, you really do not want to fuck with me, trust me on this. What you and your friends want to do right now is turn around and walk out of here. You are drunk, loud, and you are bothering us."

The sailor laughed. "You're American, too." he said. "You think we're afraid of a couple of faggots, French or American?"

Bogey turned to Jerome and spoke again in French. "When this starts, just get out of the way." Then he turned back toward the sailor and in a perfectly efficient motion with his left hand grabbed him behind the neck, and slammed his head on the bar. The sailor slumped to the floor with a groan. Nearly simultaneously, with his right hand Bogey threw a straight punch that broke the nose of the second sailor, who fell to his knees, and put both his hands over his face. "You broke my fucking nose, you son-of-a-bitch," the sailor blubbered through the flow of blood. Bogey saw that Jerome had indeed ducked out of the way, but there was no need for him to harm the third sailor, Randy, who now raised his hands plaintively.

"It's alright, sir," he said. "I don't want no trouble with you. This was all my fault to begin with. We'll get out of here right now, I'm real sorry, mister."

Bogey pulled some franc notes from his pocket, slapped them on the bar, apologized to the barman for the disturbance, and, as the sailor Randy was trying to gather up his friends on the floor, he and Jerome walked out of the bar.

"Why didn't you tell me you were queer?" Bogey asked when they were outside.

"Why would I?" asked Jerome. "What difference does it make? Did you tell me about your sexual predilections? Don't worry, you're not my type, I can spot a heterosexual a mile away."

"That's good to know, Jerome."

"The fact is, the one named Randy propositioned *me* last night," said Jerome, "and when we were about to get down to business outside behind the bar, his two friends walked up. He pretended then that I had accosted him, while in fact ours was an arrangement of entirely mutual consent."

"So how did you avoid getting your ass kicked by those three?" Bogey asked.

"I ran, of course," Jerome said. "My people have always been good runners. And I've learned that if one is homosexual, and chooses to be nonviolent, it is very helpful to be able to run fast."

6

On a dark, damp, late afternoon in mid-November, Bogey was sitting in Le Select writing in his notebook. It had begun to snow outside, and he was glad to be in the warm, snug café. The weather reminded him of the war years, when winter seemed interminable, and men were always cold. He was writing a story about a wounded German soldier he had encountered on one such afternoon. He had been delivering a dispatch, and as they often did, he and Crazy Horse had crossed German lines as the most direct path to their destination.

It was snowing that day, a wet snow turning periodically to sleet. Although Bogey wore his long canvas stockman's coat, there was no protection against the weather, which was not like the dry cold of the Colorado high country from which he came, but a heavy, invasive cold that soaked into your bones until you began to believe that you would never be warm again. Bogey rode up toward a partially destroyed farmhouse, with half the roof collapsed and the doors and windows broken out. He thought he might be able to take shelter here from the snow, but as always in such situations, he was alert to the possibility of there being enemies inside, or perhaps just a lone sniper. As he approached, he heard a man call out plaintively in German. He drew his six-shooter from the holster. The man called out again, and Bogey saw a white flag protrude from a window on the end of a rifle barrel.

Now Bogey glanced up from his notebook, and through the steamy window of Le Select his eyes met those of a young woman standing outside, looking in at him. Their gazes locked for an instant, but Bogey was still living inside his story, and he went quickly back to his notebook.

He was riding up to the partially destroyed farmhouse and the German called out to him and poked the white flag out the window at the end of his rifle. Bogey felt the familiar flood of adrenaline—the warning sign that perhaps it was a trick, and in the next instant he would die. But the German called out again, and Bogey recognized the fear in his voice, a tone of pain and desperate loneliness. He slipped his Colt back in the holster, raised both hands to show that he was unarmed, and dismounted. He walked through the doorway of the gutted farmhouse. The German was crouched on the floor beneath the window, wrapped in a thin gray wool blanket, shivering and clutching his midsection. Bogey saw that where he held himself at his waist, the blanket was saturated with blood.

"Do you speak English?" Bogey asked. The German shook his head.

"French?"

"Yes."

Bogey picked up the man's rifle, a bolt-action Mannlicher, the white flag attached to the end of the barrel. He pulled the bolt and saw that the weapon was loaded.

"Why didn't you shoot me?" he asked the German.

The soldier smiled weakly. "I thought I was hallucinating," he said. "I know who you are. It would be bad luck to kill you. I have had enough bad luck. Besides, why should both of us die?"

"What's your name?"

"Oskar. And yours?"

"Bogart."

"You must have German blood for that is a German name," said Oskar.

"No, it is French," Bogey said.

"It is French, and German. I know this for I have an uncle from Alsace named Bogart. Perhaps we are related." Oskar's teeth started chattering violently. "I am so cold Bogart," he said.

Bogey went back outside, unstrapped his bedroll from behind the saddle, and brought it into the farmhouse. He untied the thongs, unrolled the bedroll, and draped it over the man.

"Thank you," Oscar said, "thank you, you are very kind. Now I must ask you another favor."

"Alright."

"Will you stay here with me for just a little while? I am dying, I am in great pain, and I am afraid. I would like for you to stay and talk to me. And before you leave, I would like for you to shoot me in the head, so that I will not suffer any longer. Will you do that for me, please, Bogart?"

Bogey paused in his writing in Le Select on this winter day, and when he glanced up, he saw that the young woman who had been looking in from outside had taken a seat at a table across from him, and that she appeared to be sketching him. Their eyes met again and held this time, and then she looked quickly back at her sketchpad. Bogey watched her impassively for a moment; he was coming to the hard part of his story now, and he welcomed the diversion of looking at a pretty girl in real time, rather than living in the memory of these stories. He knew that this was why he wrote them; he never meant them for publication, or even for anyone else to read. He somehow believed that if he could only write down all his memories, transfer them to pieces of paper, he could leave them there, he could clear them out of his head once and for all.

The young woman looked up at him again, and saw that he was still watching her, but this time she did not look away. Rather she held his gaze in her own. She was very pretty, with dark hair under her wool hat and large deep-set eyes that seemed wise beyond her years, and slightly mischievous. She smiled slightly, and went back to her sketching, and Bogey, although he did not wish to, went back inside his story.

"I'm sorry, Oskar," he said, "but I don't think I can do that."

"But why not, Bogart? I am your enemy. That is what we are supposed to do, we are supposed to try to kill each other."

"But you did not kill me when you had the chance."

"Because if I had killed you, I could not ask you to kill me," said Oskar. "That is why I called out to you. Please, Bogart, I am begging you."

"I can't. I'm sorry, Oskar, but I just can't."

Oskar began to weep, his face in a terrible grimace.

"What did you want to talk about?" Bogey asked, by way of trying to distract him. "Tell me."

"Where do you come from, Bogart?" Oskar asked through his pain.

"Colorado."

"I have never been to America. You have mountains in Colorado, do you not?"

"Yes, my family has a small ranch in a high mountain valley in northern Colorado," Bogey said. "It is big open country of hay meadows and sage flats, and vast fields of buffalo grass that grow taller than a man's waist in the summer, and undulate in the wind like waves at sea. There are rivers, streams, and creeks running through the valley, which is surrounded on all sides by four different mountain ranges. There are trout in the rivers, and in the mountains many deer and elk."

"It must be very beautiful," Oskar said.

"Yes, it is. And where do you come from, Oskar?"

"I come from Bavaria. A small village in the mountains. It is also very beautiful. My father is a clockmaker. I, too, am a clockmaker. I am my father's apprentice."

"That seems like a fine profession, Oskar," Bogey said. "Listen, I can take you out of here. You can ride behind me on my horse. I will take you closer to your troops, where they will find you and get you to a doctor."

"I cannot ride, Bogart," Oskar said. "My guts are falling out, that is why they left me here. I am dying. Are you sure you cannot shoot me? Please, I am in such terrible pain."

Now Bogey, too, began to weep. "I am so sorry, Oskar, I just cannot do that."

"Alright, Bogart, I understand, but then I am afraid I must kill you. That is, after all, why we are here, is it not?"

From beneath the blanket, Oskar pulled a Mauser pistol, and swung it toward Bogey. Instinctively, without time to think, Bogey drew his Colt from the holster and shot Oskar through the forehead. He took the Mauser from the German's hand, knowing before he had even broken open the magazine, that it was unloaded.

Bogey closed his notebook, pulled change from his pocket, looked at the bill the waiter had left, and dropped coins on the saucer. He stood and began to walk toward the door of Le Select. He did not look at the girl again, or even think about her. He was still inside his story, and he felt hollow and sick to his stomach. But as he passed her table, she spoke to him.

"Excuse me, sir," she said, "but I made a sketch of you. Would you like to see it?"

Bogey stopped and looked at the girl, his gaze unfocused. He stared at her but he did not see, or understand, or answer her. He was still so deeply within his story, the memory so profoundly real and painful, that he had the sense that he had just now killed the apprentice clockmaker, Oskar—not seven years ago.

"I'm very sorry to disturb you, sir," she said. "I just…I just thought you might like to see the sketch I made of you while you were writing. May I…may I show it to you?"

Bogey kept staring at the girl until gradually she came back into focus. "*Non, non, merci,*" he said, shaking his head, and he went to the rack by the door, put on his coat and hat, and walked out of Le Select into the snowy winter evening.

CHRYSIS & BOGEY

1926

1

Chrysis continued her studies with Professor Humbert, and beyond the formal painting assignments for the atelier, her work began to take on an increasingly personal shape and style. It was inevitable that the unfolding discovery of her body and of her own sensuality would find its way into her paintings, and she came to understand that this was all part of the same process, that her passion for life and erotic experience translated naturally into the color, form and subject matter of her art.

Nor did she avoid exploring the darker side of eroticism, the fine line between sensuality and pornography, passion and obsession, gratification and perversion. She knew that she could not be a good artist unless she embraced all the multi-faceted contradictions inherent in the demands of the flesh, both as a blessing and as a curse.

Chrysis became fascinated by the world of prostitutes, the women for hire whom she saw in some of the bars and clubs, and whom the owners and managers of the better establishments tried to chase away. One afternoon she asked Casmir to take her to a brothel.

"What do you wish to do there?" he asked. The gypsy poet was beginning to worry that he had unleashed an inner monster in this girl, for her curiosity about all things sexual now seemed insatiable. He knew that she did not love him; indeed, she seemed far more interested in the world of eroticism than she did in their personal relationship.

"I wish to observe," she answered, "and to sketch."

And so that same evening Casmir took her to La Belle Poule (*the beautiful hen*, a French slang term for prostitute), on the rue Blondel, in the red light district of the blvd. St. Denis. It was an establishment of which the poet himself was an occasional customer in the rare times when he had a little spare money.

The proprietor, Madame Mireille, a thin, hawk-faced women, greeted them in the foyer, which was elaborately tiled in abstract mosaics. She looked Chrysis over with hard, shrewd eyes. "And what can I do for you today, my friend?" she asked Casmir. "I presume that you would like to share one of the girls with this lovely young woman of yours."

"No, as a matter of fact, madame," Casmir explained, "the young lady would simply like to avail herself of your *chambre de divertissement individual" (*individual entertainment room). This was the name of the brothel's secret voyeurism room which had two peep holes drilled through the wall, artfully disguised on the other side by a lively mural painted some years earlier, in return for services rendered, by the Mexican artist Diego Rivera, a regular customer of La Belle Poule during his time in Paris. Through these holes, those wishing to be mere spectators could peer into the adjoining "Red Room," looking through the eyes of a character in the mural, while the customer there, unaware that he was being watched, performed various and sundry acts with the girl or girls of his choice.

"And does the young lady wish to watch you with one of the girls?" the madame asked Casmir. "For business is slow at the moment and we do not currently have a customer in the Red Room."

"You may speak directly to me, madame," Chrysis said. "I am not deaf and dumb. I requested this visit here myself and I will be paying for it."

Madame Mireille arched her eyebrows, unaccustomed to girls addressing her in this manner. "Very well, young lady," she said. "Tell me, what then is your pleasure?"

"I would be delighted to watch Casmir with one of your girls," said Chrysis. "In addition I would like to choose her."

The madame led them up an elegant wrought-iron staircase to the establishment's grand salon. There the walls were decorated with antique mirrors and erotic paintings in the style of the frescoes of Pompeii—voluptuous nymphs lolling naked on fluffy clouds, while other women danced sensuously beneath them.

There was a bar against one wall, with tables and chairs, the room furnished in the ornate style of the *Belle Epoque.* Four or five young woman, dressed in various revealing outfits, lounged about, looking exceptionally bored. As it was still early in the evening, there was not a single customer in the establishment.

While Casmir and Madame Mireille had a glass of champagne at the bar, Chrysis made the rounds of the salon, looking carefully at all the girls, smiling and exchanging a word or two with each. As professionals, they were quite accustomed to being inspected like merchandise at Le Bon Marché department store, though in this case, it was rather a novelty that the prospective customer was a beautiful young woman. Chrysis chose finally a red-haired girl who appeared to be the least bored and the most animated of the group. She had an easy smile and a certain natural way about her. Chrysis also noted that the girl had a shapely figure, and she thought her red hair would be a fine addition to a painting.

"Does she please you?" Chrysis asked Casmir after she led the redhead to the bar. "But then perhaps you two already know each other."

"No, I have not yet had the pleasure," he answered, "Yes, she is lovely. And what exactly would you like me to do with her?"

Chrysis laughed. "Why, anything you wish. But first I would like to sketch her alone, if that would be acceptable to madame."

"For that activity," said Madame Mireille, "I must charge you the same rate as all other customers pay for their time with the girls, and for the use of the room."

"Of course."

2

The girl's name was Juliette, and she was a funny, lively, talkative, sexy woman, and as sometimes happens between an artist and a model, she and Chrysis seemed to develop a kind of immediate complicity. As Chrysis sketched her, Juliette told her that she came from the waterfront neighborhood of Marseille, that she had been the mistress of an important underworld figure there. But the man beat her when he drank, and the beatings became increasingly frequent until she had begun to fear for her life. One night after he had passed out, she ran away to Paris. She said she was afraid that he would come looking for her and so she changed her name and went to work for Madame Mireille, because there is a certain anonymity among prostitutes. She felt safe here with the other girls, none of whom used their real names, and all of whom had at least one story about bad men in their past.

First Chrysis made a sketch of Juliette sitting on the bed, still fully dressed as if she was waiting for the arrival of her customer, then another of her standing, with one leg on a chair, removing a stocking, and a third of her lying naked on the bed. With these sketches, Chrysis intended to do a series of paintings that she would title, *Waiting for the Client.* Juliette was an excellent model, genuinely expressive of the different moods and poses of her profession.

Now Chrysis went to sit on the edge of the bed, to arrange Juliette for the final series of sketches. "Roll over on your side," she said. As the girl did so, Chrysis noticed the scar on her hip, and she touched the raised tissue gently with her fingers. "What happened to you here."

"Look closely," Juliette said. "You will see the initials, MT. Maurice Toscan carves them into all his girls as a sign of ownership.

"But that is monstrous."

"I think that you and I must be nearly the same age," Juliette said. "But we have clearly led very different lives."

Chrysis placed her hand gently on Juliette's hip, covering the brand with her palm. "I am so sorry, Juliette."

Juliette smiled and shrugged. "That's just the way it is, isn't it? But it is done now."

"I will only make one more sketch of you," Chrysis said. "But first I must ask you a question. Does it ever happen that a customer actually satisfies you, and makes you feel something like love?"

"Very, very rarely," Juliette said. "But occasionally one does have the illusion of making love rather than a business deal, and that is always a bittersweet feeling with a customer who is paying for your services."

"For this last sketch, I would like for you to imagine such an occasion," Chrysis said. "I want you to imagine that you have just made love, and you have had an orgasm, and your lover/client has now left, and you are resting here alone, sated and content on the one hand, but at the same time with that bittersweet feeling you describe."

Juliette nodded. She took Chrysis's hand from her hip, and rolled onto her back, placing it on the warm soft spot between stomach and pubis. "But why do you ask me to imagine such a state, Chrysis? How can you make a real painting if your model is only acting, only pretending to feel something she does not truly feel in the moment?" Very slowly, she moved Chrysis's hand up her stomach to her rib cage just beneath her breast, and Chrysis did not resist. "Those other poses were easy for they are all part of my daily job and require no imagination. But what you ask now is more difficult. However, if you can make me feel that way yourself, then you will have a true painting rather than a false one. And, after all, you have paid for me, haven't you?"

The feel of Juliette's smooth skin against her own, the softness of their flesh meeting, the fullness of their lips when they kissed, the sensual roundness and comfort of two women's bodies coming together, so different than the muscular angularity of a man's physique—neither better nor worse, one from the other, only different. As members of the same sex, they knew instinctively how to give each other pleasure with hands and fingers, mouths and tongues, without awkwardness or shame, and when they had finished they lay together and they did not speak. Finally, Chrysis slipped out of the bed and took up her sketchpad and drew Juliette in just that state she had described, and as she was in the same state herself, artist and model were completely one, both physically and emotionally. Chrysis recognized this as the truest, rarest kind of artistic fulfillment, one she had never experienced before, and knew would be hard to ever duplicate again.

By the time they returned to the salon, the establishment had filled with customers, the lights were low, and the atmosphere charged with that specific spirit of the brothel's erotic permissiveness. A Negro musician played jazz on the piano and clients danced with the girls on the small floor beside the bar. Chrysis found Casmir slumped in a gilded Louis XIV armchair, looking bored and irritated. She apologized to him for being so long, explaining that she had made more sketches than she had planned.

The poet laughed. "Ah, my dear, there are no secrets between us," he said. "I can smell her on you. And I can see in your languid eyes that you are sated."

"I think that I am no longer so interested in voyeurism tonight," Chrysis said. "I believe I shall simply have a glass of champagne at the bar, and settle my account with madame. And then I must return to my studio and paint. I'm very sorry Casmir."

"Don't mention it, my dear," he said. "You may simply buy me a good dinner."

Approaching the bar, Chrysis found Madame Mireille in close conference with the barman. The madame glanced at her. "I will be right with you, young lady," she said.

Chrysis looked then at the barman, who in that same moment looked over madame's shoulder, his dark eyes locking on hers. Chrysis felt suddenly lightheaded, and before she could think, she blurted out: "*But what are you doing here?*"

"I beg your pardon, mademoiselle?" said Madame Mireille.

"Forgive me, madame," Chrysis said. "I was addressing the gentleman. I didn't mean to interrupt you. I am just so surprised to see him."

"You two know each other?" madame asked.

"No, not exactly," Chrysis said. "That is to say, we have never actually met…though we know each other in a sense."

"Well then, permit me to properly introduce you," said madame, clearly confused. "This is Bogart, our new part-time bartender and full-time keeper of the peace. With all the American sailors in town, La Belle Poule is becoming a bit more…shall we say…*unruly*, than is normal with our regular clientele. I was complaining about it recently to my dear friend, Jimmie Charters, the barman at the Dingo, and he said he had just the man to fill the position. I'm afraid that I do not know your name, young lady?"

"Chrysis," she said, holding her hand out to Bogey. "I'm Chrysis,"

His grip was warm and strong, and he held Chrysis's hand in his for a long moment until she felt dizzy again. "Real pleased to meet you, miss," he said. "To answer your question, I work here. My first night." He smiled wryly. "But I might ask you the same thing."

"This is my friend, Casmir," Chrysis said, aware that she was blushing deeply.

"Bogart, let us have champagne for my friends Chrysis and Casmir," said Madame Mireille, "and perhaps you can all sort this out. Your session with Juliette was satisfactory I trust, young lady?"

"Very much so, thank you, madame."

"I must now attend to my clients," said the proprietress, moving away from the bar. "You may leave the fee upon which we agreed with Bogart, mademoiselle."

Later, Chrysis would remember that the piano man was playing and singing a new song she had heard the band play at Le Bal Nègre. It was by the American composer, Cole Porter, who lived in Paris and was a regular habitué of that establishment, and who often played with the band there himself. The song was called "*Let's Misbehave*."

"And to answer *your* question, I am working here, as well," Chrysis said to Bogey, still bewildered by his presence, and somehow feeling the need to justify herself to him. "I mean to say I…I am not obviously one of the girls…no, I do not work here in that capacity. I just came for the first time tonight to make some drawings. You see, I am a painter…and, and…my friend Casmir is a poet. But we are not in love, you understand, we are just friends…but then…why am I telling you all this? Why would you care if we are in love?…I'm sorry, I'm babbling like an idiot…please forgive me."

"I was just playing with you, miss," Bogey said, smiling at her awkwardness. "It's none of my business why you are here. And you don't have to explain anything to me."

"Will you meet me tomorrow afternoon at Le Select?" she asked. "About 4:00 p.m.? I must speak to you. I promise I won't behave so peculiarly. I'm just a little flustered…I'm just so surprised to see you…"

Bogey nodded and smiled. "Four o'clock, Le Select, I'll be there."

As they were leaving La Belle Poule, Casmir said: "That is the man you are in love with, is it not?"

"How did you know?"

Casmir just laughed.

3

"Do you remember me?" Chrysis asked.

"Yes, one evening last winter," Bogey said. "It was snowing. I was sitting at this same table writing in my notebook. And you were outside peering in the window. You looked like a cold, homeless waif."

"I have been looking for you ever since. I thought I would never see you again."

"La Belle Poule is an odd place to run into each other."

"Tell me the truth," Chrysis said, "did you ever look for me? Did you ever think about me?"

"I regretted later that I did not speak to you," Bogey said. "And that I did not look at your drawing. I was a little distracted that evening."

"I could see that. You looked like you were living in a different world than the rest of us."

"Yes, I was."

Their eyes locked then, and it seemed as though they had always known each other, that each of them already knew everything about the other, although, of course, neither knew anything.

"You are a writer," Chrysis said finally.

"No, not really," Bogey answered. "But you are a painter."

"Yes…at least I am a student of painting. I still have much to learn. You are American?"

"That's right." He smiled. "How did you ever guess?"

"Your accent gives you away. And, of course, your cowboy boots."

Bogey laughed. "Sometimes students from L'École des Beaux-Arts stop me on the sidewalk and ask me if I'm a real cowboy, or if I'm going to a costume ball."

"And how do you answer?"

"I tell them I'm going to a costume ball, of course."

"If I may ask, how does an American cowboy come to be working in a bordello in Paris?"

"That is rather a long story."

"I imagine it is. What is your real name?"

"Bogart. Bogart Lambert. But most people call me Bogey."

Chrysis looked hard at him now, a distant memory from her childhood rising as an icy shiver up her spine. "Where in America do you come from?"

"The state of Colorado. My family has a small ranch there."

"You were in the Foreign Legion."

"How do you know that?"

"I thought you were dead?"

"I beg your pardon?"

"Bogart Lambert was killed in the war," Chrysis said, "the *Boches* killed him. Papa said so."

"Who is Papa?" Bogey asked.

"My father. He told me about you and Crazy Horse," she said. "You are the cowboy courier. He told me all about you. He met you."

"Who is your father?" he asked again.

"Colonel Charles Jungbluth," she answered. "Commandant of the 217th infantry. You rode into their trenches during *La Bataille des Monts,* the spring offensive of 1917. Is that not correct?"

Bogey stared at her for a long time, and then he looked away, as if retreating back into himself. Chrysis could see again in the depths of his eyes all the anguish of remembrance she had seen that day at Le Select.

Finally, he nodded. "Yes, I remember your father. That was one of my early missions. I was so young and foolish. I believed I was invincible…bulletproof. Your father was very kind to me."

"You're not dead, after all," she said.

"I don't think so."

"All these years, ever since I was a little girl, I've believed you were dead."

"Many people believe so," Bogey said.

"Will you come to my parents' house with me?" Chrysis asked. "Will you come there with me right now? It would be such a wonderful surprise for Papa. He, too, has thought you were dead all these years. It would be a new end to the story, a wonderful new end. And such a beautiful gift I could give him."

"What story?"

"The good war story he told me when I was a little girl," she said. "The story about the cowboy courier."

"I would be pleased to see your father again," Bogey said. "But I must go to work soon. I'm off tomorrow, and if you like, I can go there with you then. But you must promise me one thing. You must promise that you will not tell anyone else about me."

"Alright, I promise," Chrysis said. "But why?"

"Because you are right about one thing," Bogey said. "The cowboy courier is dead, and I wish for him to rest in peace."

Chrysis reached out and took Bogey's hand in hers. "Bogart?"

"Yes, Chrysis."

"Do you feel that? Do you feel that between us?"

Bogey nodded.

"I have been in love with you since I was twelve years old," she said.

"You were in love with a mythical character your father created for you."

"But then I fell in love with you last year, right here," Chrysis said, "without even knowing who you were, without even speaking to you. When I saw you last night, I was still in love with you. And maybe you don't know this yet, but you are in love with me."

"I don't know much about love," said Bogey.

4

"Perhaps we should not tell father where we met the other night," Chrysis said as she was opening the door to the apartment.

Bogey laughed. "I think that's a fine idea. I remember your father as being a man of strong character."

"That is one way of putting it," she said. "I will simply say that we met at Le Select. Which is more or less true."

"Where do you tell him you make those sketches of yours?"

"I do not show them to him. At least, not yet. But one day I will."

Her parents were having an *aperitif* when Chrysis entered their salon with Bogey. The colonel stood and she kissed him, and then her mother. "I brought a friend home to see you, Papa," she said. "Someone you might remember."

The colonel's hair had turned mostly gray over the past years, and his former handlebar moustache was now neatly trimmed. He was a distinguished looking gentleman in his late fifties, still slender and with an erect military carriage. He looked quizzically at Bogey. "Have we met, then?" he asked, holding out his hand. "I'm sorry, but I am afraid that I do not recognize you."

"Yes, Colonel Jungbluth," Bogey said, raising his own hand in a salute. "We have met. I was Legionnaire 1st Class Bogart Lambert, sir, of the 4th battalion under the command of Colonel Jacques Daumier. We met briefly during the war. However, there is no reason why you should remember me."

The colonel looked closely then at Bogey, and his lower lip began to tremble. "I attended a memorial service for you," he whispered in a hoarse voice, his hand shaking as he lifted it in a salute. "You were awarded the *Croix de Guerre* posthumously for your heroic service to our country."

"Yes, sir, it was sent home to my folks in Colorado," Bogey said. "They put it in my room with my rodeo trophies."

"As your body was never found, an inquiry was held," said the colonel. "There were some in the military tribunal who believed you had deserted. However, your commanding officer and others in the battalion testified on your behalf. There were so many dead, so many buried in the field, so many simply vanished, that there was no way of knowing what had become of you. But this is remarkable. Is the Legion aware that you are still living?"

"No, Colonel," Bogey said, "nor do I have any intention of notifying them."

"But why?" asked Colonel Jungbluth. "At the very least, you will be eligible for some kind of financial compensation from the government. And the nation will honor you."

"Yes, sir, that is exactly the reason," Bogey said. "You were there, Colonel, you know what it was like. Why would I wish to bring all that up again? Why would I wish that kind of attention? The war ended seven years ago, the cowboy courier died and is forgotten. The world has moved on. I have moved on. Let us leave it at that.

Your daughter has promised not to speak of me to others. And I ask you to do the same."

The colonel considered what Bogey had said for a moment, and then he nodded. "Very well, Legionnaire Lambert. If you wish to remain a dead man, I must respect your decision. However, I would be grateful if you would do me the honor of telling us privately what happened to you, and where you have been these past years. After our brief meeting that spring, I followed your military career as closely as I was able under the circumstances. I heard many tales of your exploits."

"Wildly exaggerated, Colonel, I can assure you," Bogey said. "But yes, if you like, I will tell you what I know, what I remember, and where I have been."

And so Bogey stayed for dinner with the Jungbluth family, and he told them everything, he told them of the explosion on the road to Mons, of waking out of his long sleep in Edinburgh, the many months of surgeries and years of rehabilitation, of his boxing career in Scotland, and finally of his return to France. It occurred to him during the telling, that this was the first time he had recounted all of this in such detail to anyone. Even during the three years he had spent working with Archie, he had never confided in him in anything but the most general way, and for his part Archie had respected his privacy.

"But do you not wish to return to your home?" asked the colonel. "To see your mother and father?"

"I write my parents every week, Colonel," Bogey said, "and one day I will go home. But for some reason I cannot fully explain, I am not ready yet. My father is getting older and before too long he will need me even more on the ranch, and eventually I will take it over completely.

And when I do go back, I imagine that I will never leave there again. I am just not ready yet, and I think they understand that."

Chrysis and Bogey looked at each other then, and they both glimpsed in that moment the separate paths of their respective lives, as if the entire course of their nascent relationship lay clear ahead, and yet already behind them.

5

Chrysis was completing her second year under the tutelage of Humbert, and her work was taking on a new maturity and confidence. Despite the academic nature of painting figures in class, she continued to develop her own distinct style. This had been greatly informed and enhanced by her extracurricular work, both at the bordello and in the life of the neighborhood. These drawings and studies, and the paintings she would eventually make of them, displayed her own youthful *joie de vivre* and sensuality. They were lively, full of color, motion and gaiety. Even those with a certain darker tone that portrayed some hint of the other side of eroticism, some suggestion of the potential abyss of despair into which it might descend, even those seemed to maintain an ultimate aura of hope, of salvation.

Gradually, she had begun to show Professor Humbert some of the pieces she had done outside the atelier, those depicting real life and real people. The professor did not need to ask where these drawings and paintings had been created, nor was it his position to do so. Over the years, he had instructed a number of male students who had been briefly seduced by the thematic world of Toulouse Lautrec, but it was usually derivative on their part, a kind of homage, rather than a genuine personal passion. He recognized in the work of this sometimes troublesome young woman, the stab of actuality.

In the course of his long teaching career, Humbert had come to view his women students first as eggs, and he the brood hen who sat on the nest. Soon they became hungry young hatchlings with greedy open mouths and shrill chirps, demanding to be nourished. Then they were fledglings, making, one by one, their first tentative flights. And finally, those who had survived all of this, who had not died in the nest, or fallen out and been devoured by cats, became fully formed adults who no longer needed their mother for protection and sustenance; they flew away then once and for all, in most cases never to be seen again by the professor. For all her youth, the Jungbluth girl had been the first out of the shell, the most demanding mouth to be fed, and the first to fly, however awkwardly.

Bogey continued to work at La Belle Poule. It was not a difficult job, and reminded him of his days at Mona's in New York. He had learned a good deal about bartending from Jimmie Charters at the Dingo, and here at the bordello he shared these duties with Madame Mireille's husband, whom everyone called Père Jean, a cheerful, leprechaunish old fellow. He and Bogey made an efficient pair behind the bar, as Père Jean was utterly non-threatening to miscreant customers, and could often cajole them out of their bad behavior or temper with his own natural good cheer. And when that failed, Bogey could step in as the house "muscle."

For the most part, the American sailors, though often rowdy and loud, were not so much trouble. Bogey was struck by how young the majority of them seemed. Of course, they often drank too much, but he had had plenty of practice dealing with drunks. He did not, however, fool around with the girls at La Belle Poule as he had at Mona's, for this had not been something offered by Madame Mireille as part of his pay package, and in any case, he was in love.

Chrysis came often to the brothel in the afternoons after she had finished class at the atelier, ostensibly to sketch, but also to see Bogey, although, because he was an employee on duty, Madame Mireille did not permit them to socialize other than as bartender and customer. Chrysis had managed, finally, to become rather friendly with the old madame, who was well aware that the two were romantically involved, and who, beneath her shrewish exterior, owned a surprisingly sentimental nature. In the business of selling the illusion of love, she had a soft spot in her heart for the real thing.

On Bogey's days off, he and Chrysis sometimes went out to restaurants or cafés, or they would just wander the streets of Paris together, arm in arm, both of them tall and lanky, walking in perfect step with their long strides, only a slight limp any longer in Bogey's. They made a handsome couple, and all who saw the young lovers would smile at the sight of two people so happy together, so much in love.

One day in early October, with the leaves on the trees of Paris in full color, they were walking across the Petit Pont to the Île de la Cité, when Chrysis suddenly stopped and turned to Bogey. She took him by the shoulders, drew him close to her, and looked him hard in the eyes. "Alright, now you must tell me," she said, "what is the matter? Is it that you are still a virgin?"

Bogey laughed. "I would be a bit old for that, wouldn't I?"

"Then why have you not yet tried to seduce me? Do you not find me desirable in that way?"

"You are the most desirable woman I have ever known," he said.

"Then why?"

Bogey looked down at a barge passing on the river beneath. "I've been wanting to talk to you about this," he said. "That night I told you and your family about the explosion, and about the operations I had on my legs. They are badly disfigured, and I still have pieces of shrapnel in them that I will carry for the rest of my life. I do not want you to see them. I'm afraid they will disgust you."

"And that is the only reason?" she asked. "Everything else is in order?"

"Yes, as far as I know, everything else is in perfect working condition."

"But you're crazy!" she said. "I thought either you didn't want me, or you had other injuries. Or you were simply shy. I've been waiting for you. Why didn't you just tell me this? Don't you understand that I don't care what your legs look like? Did you really imagine that we were going to be in love, but that you would never take your pants off in front of me?"

Bogey laughed, both amused by Chrysis, and embarrassed at his own reticence. "It is true that I've been trying to figure out some way around that," he admitted.

"Listen to me," she said, "there is no way around it. But now I must tell you something about myself, Bogey. I must be honest with you. I am not a virgin."

"From what I understand, sweetheart," Bogey said with a gentle smile, "as of this year, 1926, there are officially no longer any virgins in Paris."

That afternoon, Bogey took her back to his apartment, which he had furnished like a ranch hand's bunkhouse back home, with simple wood furniture, an iron bed frame, and a small wood kitchen stove.

"You are so tidy for a man," Chrysis said. "I would be embarrassed for you to see my studio. I am not nearly so neat. In fact, I'm rather a mess."

Bogey took her hand in his and raised it to his lips. "I already knew that about you, my darling," he said. "But I like that you always have paint on your hands and under your fingernails." He drew her index finger across his mouth. He unbuttoned her blouse and kissed her neck. She had specks of paint on her chest which flushed red now. He lifted her top over her head; she raised her arms and he pulled it off. There was paint on her breasts, as well. "You are painting in primary colors," he whispered, kissing her there, "and nude."

"A freedom not permitted in Humbert's atelier," she said. "But I believe that if the models expose themselves, so should the painter be willing to. It creates a sense of equality, and of intimacy."

Bogey knelt at her feet, slipped off her Moroccan slippers, and stroked her bare ankles. He seemed so strong, calm, and self-contained that she gladly gave herself over to him, and in so doing her own passivity aroused her. He untied the drawstring of her pantaloons and slipped then down over her hips and off her legs. Then he stood, unbuttoned his own shirt and peeled it off, revealing the corded muscles of his arms and torso, a boxer's physique, scarred by war and fights. He unbuckled his belt and stepped out of his jeans. Now they both stood naked, looking into each other's eyes, lost in the mist of the sweet longing of love. Bogey took her in his arms and she felt his strong chest against her breasts, his erect sex warm on her stomach. And he felt her breasts firm against his chest, her stomach warm on his sex; in this way they fit together as if one's sensation belonged to the other.

In bed they took time exploring each other, touching, kissing, holding close; warmth against warmth, skin against skin. She ran her hand gently down his leg, feeling the knots of scar tissue, the craters of missing flesh and muscle. Bogey flinched at first at her touch, not out of pain, which was mostly over now, but out of the memory of pain, and out of apprehension. He had not been with a woman since the night before he left Mona's and sailed from New York ten years ago, and other than the nurses at the hospital, none had seen or touched his legs. Chrysis felt his body stiffen slightly and she whispered, "It's alright, it's fine, you're beautiful, I love you," and she stroked his wounded legs until he began to believe her and relaxed again. And then there was nothing they could not do with each other, to each other, no pleasure denied, nothing forbidden, no part unexplored; they owned each other's bodies in a kind of intimacy neither had ever known before, and their orgasm as they looked again into each others' eyes, seemed to be one shared between them, fusing them together until they became one being, perfect and complete.

Later, enveloped by the soft evening air of autumn, they walked arm and arm in silence through the narrow streets of the *quartier,* the street lights just coming on, past the cafés, bars and restaurants, their terraces beginning to fill with people taking their daily aperitif. And now those who witnessed the young couple recognized the glow of spent passion on their faces, and all smiled slyly, knowingly, grateful to share in the aftermath of their lovemaking.

CHRYSIS & BOGEY

1927

1

And so Chrysis divided her time between her studies at the Atelier Humbert, her blossoming love affair with the American cowboy, her familial responsibilities as dutiful daughter, and her still secret life as both artist and participant in the soft, seductive underbelly of Parisian nightlife. She moved confidently between these worlds with the grace of youth, in love with all of the varied and seemingly contradictory components of her life. She loved her work with Professor Humbert; although he was becoming ever more cantankerous with age, they had largely made their peace together, and she felt now a tremendous fondness for the old man. She loved her mother, Marie-Reine, at heart a lively, gay woman but one whose true nature had been suppressed by a lifetime under the rule of her husband, the colonel. She loved her father, admired, and even feared him at times. Yet despite his severity, she knew how much he had sacrificed in order to give her the opportunity to pursue her artistic dreams. And, of course, she loved her quiet, troubled cowboy, Bogey Lambert, the only person she had ever known who did not appear to be in the least bit intimidated by the colonel. This intrigued Chrysis and attracted her even more to Bogey, a man whose integrity and simple strength of character was the rare equal of her father's. And yet she also recognized in him a certain fragility, a gentle nature that deepened and enriched their intimacy.

Beyond her personal and professional relationships, Chrysis loved the vibrant world of Montparnasse, this international coming together of artists in a common spirit of liberation, fueling the life of the cafés, the bars, the cabarets, the balls and bordellos—endless energy and constant motion, mystery and sensual excitement. Chrysis loved all of it, she felt like the luckiest young woman on earth to experience all this richness, all this adventure. In this way, the weeks and the months passed, youth hurtling by as it does with such speed, force and alacrity that one is unaware, until it is over, that it does not last forever.

Because she had classes with the professor most mornings, and was under the watchful eyes of her parents at night, Chrysis was not often able to go La Belle Poule to sketch late at night or in the early hours of the morning. Only when her parents were in the countryside was she free to slip away, and she found that the atmosphere in the brothel was truest during these witching hours after midnight. It was a softer, richer, more reflective time, sometimes of great gaiety and other times of pathos, a time when everyone shed their inhibitions and exposed their true selves. It was just this spirit of openness that Chrysis hoped to capture in her work.

On one such late spring night while she was sketching in the main salon, the painter Jules Pascin, a regular client, came in with his entourage of friends and hangers-on, all of them rather drunk. Wearing his trademark bowler hat, white scarf and black suit, with a cigarette dangling from his mouth, Pascin surveyed the salon. Madame came over to Chrysis and asked her to put away her sketchpad, out of respect to the "house" artist.

In the process of selecting girls with whom to drink champagne and dance, the painter noticed Chrysis. "Do I not recognize you from the cafés of the village, young lady?" he asked. "I am a little drunk and I am afraid that I have forgotten your name…or indeed, even if I have ever known it. What, may I ask, are you doing in this place?"

"Working, Monsieur Pascin," Chrysis answered. "And my name is Chrysis."

"Splendid, Chrysis!" said Pascin. "In that case, consider yourself hired. Let us dance!"

Chrysis laughed. "Not that kind of work, sir," she said. "I, too, am a painter and Madame Mirelle sometimes allows me to sketch here. However, she instructed me to put away my pad when you entered, for she says that you, and you alone, are the resident artist of La Belle Poule."

"I cannot tell you how immensely proud that makes me," Pascin said. "I shall insist the legend be engraved upon my headstone! And, indeed, there shall be a large bonus at the end of the night for madame." He handed Chrysis his calling card. "Yes, now I recall seeing you sketching in the cafés. Come to my studio tomorrow. I will give you work as a model. You are really quite lovely, and I should like to dress you and paint you."

"Ah, yes, I have admired your paintings in the galleries, Monsieur Pascin," she said, "and I have seen how you like to dress your models. But I'm afraid that I do not do that kind of work, either. If I occasionally pose, it is only for my own paintings.

"But anyone in the neighborhood can tell you that I pay my models more than any of the other artists," Pascin said.

"And I'm told that you ask more of them, as well."

"You are a cheeky young thing, aren't you?"

"Perhaps you would like to model for me, Monsieur Pascin?" Chrysis asked. "Male artists are always painting nude women, but no one seems any longer to paint nude men, except as studies in the ateliers, or as tests of figurative technique for *Le Prix de Rome* competition."

Pascin laughed. "That is because no dealers will buy paintings of nude men," he said. "Least of all nude paintings of me. A simple matter of aesthetics and the marketplace. In any case, I, too, am strictly a painter, and not a model."

"Good, then we are equals," Chrysis said.

"Cheeky, indeed! What did you say your name was?"

"Chrysis. Chrysis Jungbluth."

"And have you exhibited your work, Mademoiselle Jungbluth?"

"Not yet, sir, I am still a student at the Atelier Humbert."

"Perhaps one day when you are ready for an exhibition," said Pascin, "I might be able to assist you. In the meantime, let us have a glass of champagne together, and you may show me some of your drawings."

Bogey delivered a bottle of champagne and glasses on a tray to Pascin's table. He and Chrysis smiled secretly at one another as she opened her sketchpad to show the painter her work. Madame Mireille looked on, pleased that the two artists had struck up a cordial relationship, and proud that her establishment was once again providing this timeless link between sex and art, neither of which, in her opinion, could exist without the other.

"Not bad," said Pascin, flipping the pages. "Yes, quite interesting work. I assumed that you must have some talent or you would not dare be so cheeky. Tell me, in what other mediums do you work?"

"Primarily oil and watercolor."

"Excellent. You must come by my studio some day with more of your paintings. I promise that I shall not ask you to model…or perform any of the other services of which you speak."

The bell rang, announcing the arrival of more early morning customers, and Madame Mireille went downstairs to greet them. At this hour, she rarely admitted anyone other than regular clients, but now she returned with three men. As the men entered the salon, they seemed to bring an icy winter draft with them through the door, the atmosphere changing instantly from one of warm, relaxed early hours decadence to one of ominous menace. Madame Mireille's face looked drawn and pale, and she cut a worried glance toward Bogey at the bar. The men wore dark overcoats and fedoras and they looked as though they came from out of town. The two men in the rear appeared to be bodyguards of the man in front, and they held their hands in the pockets of their overcoats.

"Good evening, ladies and gentlemen," said the lead man, removing his hat and tipping it gallantly. "Please, allow me to introduce myself. I am Maurice Toscan, and these are my colleagues. But please, pay us no mind, continue your revelry. We are simply here on a brief mission, which, upon successful completion, will result in our leaving as quietly and as peacefully as we have come." The man surveyed the salon. "I am looking for a young lady by the name of Ariane Rampal, whom I have reason to believe is an employee in this *distinguished* establishment. To any of you regular customers, or any of you girls, she would be easily identifiable for having the intials MT engraved upon her lovely ass."

"I have already explained to monsieur," said Madame Mireille, still looking at Bogey, "that there is no one by that name or description employed here."

"Well, then, I am afraid that we shall have to search the rooms," Toscan said. "I am terribly sorry to inconvenience you all in this manner."

Just then Juliette came down the staircase and into the salon with her most recent customer. She froze when she saw the man, the color draining from her face.

"My darling Ariane," Toscan said. "I have found you at last."

"You need not harm anyone here, Maurice," Juliette said. "I will come with you quietly, but first you must give me a few minutes to gather my affairs."

"But of course, my love," he said, and he turned to one of his thugs, "Gérard, go with Ariane to help her pack."

"I do not require Gérard's help, Maurice," Juliette said. "I am quite capable of packing myself."

"But my darling," said Toscan, "love of my life, what if you slipped away out a back door, and I were to lose you once again? No, no, I simply could not bear it. I have searched so long for you, and now, finally, we are reunited. You do understand my position, don't you, darling?"

"Yes, Maurice, I understand."

"Go with her now, Gérard. And madame, while we are waiting, and for the inconvenience we have caused, let us have champagne for the house." Toscan raised his hand and snapped his fingers. "Bartender," he called across the room, "champagne for all my friends! Piano man, play some music!"

Père Jean busied himself opening champagne bottles, while Bogey prepared trays behind the bar. Unseen by the men, he strapped on his gun belt. Then walking casually across the room, he brought a tray with a bottle and several glasses to Toscan, who had taken a seat at a table, while his second bodyguard continued to stand watch by the door, one hand still in the pocket of his overcoat.

"What the hell is that you're wearing, bartender?" Toscan demanded.

"Oh, that, sir?" Bogey said as he set the tray on the table. "Nothing to worry about, sir. I am only a costume cowboy, and this is just a toy gun, a prop. You see, we have theme nights here at La Belle Poule, when the staff and the girls dress up in various outfits for the amusement of the clients. Friday is cowboy and Indian night, and as you can see, I am playing the role of cowboy. But I'm afraid that at this hour all the Indians have already gone home."

"Give me that gun," Toscan said. "Remove it very slowly from the holster with your thumb and forefinger, and hand it over to me.

"I beg your pardon, sir?"

"You heard me, cowboy, hand me the fucking gun. You have five seconds before my man Luc shoots you dead." Luc pulled his gun from his coat pocket and pointed it at Bogey. "I can assure you, he does not miss. *One…two…*"

"Of course, no problem, sir," Bogey said, and just as Toscan said, "*three,*" Bogey drew his Colt and shot the bodyguard through the throat. Several of the girls cried out in terror at the deafening report of the gun in the room, the shattering act of violence. Luc dropped his weapon, took hold of his neck with both hands, blood pouring through his fingers. He dropped to his knees and fell over. Bogey already had the barrel of his gun against Toscan's temple. "You need to count faster, Maurice," he said. "Now put both your hands on the table, and if you move a muscle, I'll blow your brains out with my toy gun."

"My other man is going to come down those stairs any minute now," Toscan said.

"Yes, I know that," said Bogey, slipping his hand inside the man's coat and removing a pistol from a shoulder holster. "But it's going to take him a moment to get his clothes on again, because you know what Gerard is doing right now, don't you, Maurice? He's fucking your girlfriend."

"You have no idea who I am, cowboy," said Maurice. "And you have no idea of the trouble you are in."

"I know exactly who you are," Bogey said. "You're the piece of shit gangster who carves his initials into women."

Now everyone heard Gérard charging down the stairs, and when he reached the last step, he flattened against the inside wall of the stairwell. Then, gun leveled, he stepped into the doorway, and in the split-second before he could assess the situation, Bogey shot him through the heart. In that moment of distraction, Toscan drew a knife from his sleeve, and Chrysis called out just as he lunged at Bogey, stabbing him in the side. Bogey struck Toscan in the temple with the butt of his Colt, knocking him to the floor. He trained the gun on him again.

"You know what we say in the Wild West, don't you, Maurice?" Bogey asked, holding his side with his other hand as a dark stain of blood spread across his waist. "Never come to a gunfight armed only with a knife." He pulled the trigger, shooting Toscan between the eyes at point-blank range.

2

Alerted by the gunfire, the police arrived quickly, followed shortly thereafter by an ambulance which transported Bogey to the hospital. Chrysis rode with him. Thanks to her having cried out in warning, and his own reflexes, he had turned his body just enough that instead of being stabbed directly in the back and possibly through a vital organ, the knife blade had only entered the flesh of his side. At the hospital, the doctor cleaned, stitched, wrapped the wound, and sent him home.

A police inquiry was held, and the assailants identified as criminals from the Marseille waterfront, their leader, Maurice Toscan, a particularly notorious underworld figure there. Jules Pascin, as well as others present that night, were called to give testimony, and Bogey's shooting of Toscan was ruled an act of self-defense. In order not to call attention either to Paris or La Belle Poule, which might encourage members of Toscan's gang in Marseille to seek vengeance, the police concealed the incident from the press, and the men's bodies were quietly buried in unmarked graves in a pauper's cemetery outside the city.

Chrysis was badly shaken by the events of the night, and for a long time after she had nightmares about it. Suddenly, what she had always naively perceived as the carefree, libertine world of Parisian nightlife—with only a titillating potential for danger—had taken on a violent and terrifying reality. The experience caused her to recall certain dark scenes in the novel *Aphrodite*; the obsessive crimes and punishment of erotic attraction, the evil of which men and women are capable in the name of love. She could not stop replaying the scene in her mind, or questioning Bogey about it.

"How did you know what that man Gérard was doing upstairs with Juliette?" she asked.

"I didn't know," he answered. "I just said it to throw Toscan off balance, to give him something else to think about. It's an old boxing tactic."

"What would you have done if he hadn't come at you with the knife? Would you have killed him anyway?"

"No, that would have been an execution," Bogey said. "But I assumed he was carrying another weapon of some sort. And I was hoping he would try something, just to give me a legitimate excuse to kill him. Otherwise, he would have come back, and things would have been a lot worse for everyone."

"And it does not bother you to kill people?"

"I doesn't bother me to kill bad men who are trying to kill me, or others around me." Bogey said. "But during the war, I had to kill men who weren't bad, they were just on the other side. Yes, that bothers me."

"How did you learn how to do such things?" Chrysis asked.

"My father taught me to defend myself at a young age," he answered. "He taught me how to box, and quick-draw shoot. I began competing in county fairs when I was eleven years old. And now I have been to war, where I learned to do other things I wish I hadn't."

"You have lived rather a violent life, haven't you, Bogey?" Chrysis asked. "Guns, boxing, war, working as a bouncer, killing people? And yet you are such a gentle man in all other ways. Have you ever wondered if you are attracted to violence, if perhaps you seek it out? If perhaps you like it?"

"Yes, Chrysis, I have wondered that," he said. "The war changed something inside me. It made me angry. I noticed it when I started boxing again. I didn't only want to win, as I had formerly; I wanted to punish my opponents, I wanted to hurt them. That in turn made me feel shame, which is one reason I gave it up. But why do you ask me such questions?"

"I'm not sure. I suppose just to know more about you. To better understand the world you live in."

"You already know everything about me, sweetheart," Bogey said. "And we live in the same world, you and I, we just play different roles in it. It is a terrifying, dangerous place, and not one we are always able to understand. If I had not been at the brothel that night, those three men would still be alive, and your friend Juliette would likely be dead by now. So yes, in that regard I liked killing Toscan, because he was a bad man who deserved to die."

"Juliette once told me that if Maurice Toscan ever found her, he would either kill her or she would kill herself," Chrysis said. "It is true that you saved her life. You see, I was glad you killed those men, myself, I was glad to see them die. And that is something I cannot forget, and which makes me feel shame."

"We have instincts as human beings, as animals, to protect ourselves and our loved ones," Bogey said. "Sometimes under close examination these seem dark, ugly. But frequently they keep us alive. Now let's not talk about this any longer."

Chrysis laughed. "Bogey, you remind me sometimes of my father, who never wants to discuss unpleasant subjects. Indeed, the only story he ever told me about the war was the one about the cowboy courier. You men always try to bury your true feelings, while we women like to dig them up, expose them to the light of day."

"I write mine down in my notebooks," Bogey said. "That is how I dig them up."

"No," Chrysis said, "that is how you try to bury them."

3

Colonel and Madame Jungbluth were well aware of the burgeoning romance between their daughter and Bogart Lambert, and for the most part they approved of it. Chrysis regularly brought Bogey home to dine with her parents. They found him to be a polite, respectful, intelligent young man, and he and the colonel had in common the unspoken bond of their war experience. After these dinners, her father enjoyed retiring to his study with Bogey to smoke and share a cognac. Chrysis always wondered what they discussed there and when she asked Bogey, he answered: "the weather, politics, art, books, horses, the countryside, fishing, hunting, that kind of thing. Your father likes to hear about Colorado."

"Do you ever talk about the war?"

"Never."

"Why not?"

"Because we both already know what it was like."

"Does he ever ask you about us?"

"No." Bogey laughed. "You really are nosy, aren't you?

"You know that perfectly well about me," Chrysis said, laughing herself. "I must know everything! I used to drive my father crazy asking him questions. But he loves me, and one of these days, he will ask you what your intentions are toward his only daughter."

"Yes, I imagine he will."

"And how will you answer?"

"With the truth," Bogey said. "I will tell him that I hope to spend the rest of my life with his daughter, but that we haven't quite worked out the details yet."

"It is complicated, isn't it, Bogey?"

"Yes."

Chrysis accompanied her parents to the seaside in Brittany for six weeks that summer. She and her father went out sketching *en plein air* nearly every day, as they had since she was a child. By now the colonel could clearly see that his daughter had long since surpassed him in terms of artistic technique, although landscape was still not her preferred subject matter. "You are more like your mother in this regard," the colonel pointed out. "More sociable than I. And it shows in your work. You prefer being in the company of others, while I prefer the solitude of the countryside."

One day as they worked by the sea, the colonel finally did bring up the subject of Bogey. "In less than six months you will reach your majority, my daughter," he said. "Tell me, have you and Bogart made any plans together for the future?"

"No, Papa," she answered, "I wish to finish my studies with Professor Humbert first. Are you already worried that your daughter is going to be an old maid?"

"Quite the contrary, my dear," said the colonel. "I am worried my only child is going to run off to the wilds of Colorado, and that I shall never see her again. Bogart is a fine young man, and as I think you know, I have grown quite fond of him. However, it is difficult for me to imagine you in the role of rancher's wife. Just as it is difficult for me to imagine your mother's and my life in France without you."

"Then do not imagine it, Papa," Chrysis said, "for no such plans have even been discussed between us."

"I believe that Bogart wishes to return home soon," said the colonel. "He speaks to me often of his parents and the ranch. He has been in Europe now for over a decade, and I can see that he grows increasingly restless and homesick. You tell me he works as a barman which is hardly satisfactory work for a young man of his quality and background, nor one that I imagine him continuing forever. And you tell me that he writes, but then everyone in Montparnasse paints or writes these days, is that not so? At the same time, I have seen during these past two years how close the two of you have grown, how you have blossomed together. You have matured, your talent has been enriched, and you seem to have brought Bogart out of his shell, opened him up in some essential way. I have seen other wounded soldiers healed by love, and for that I give you great credit. What you have together is a fine thing to witness between a man and a woman. Yet it is also worrisome. I believe that he stays here in France for you. But inevitably he must move on with his life, and in the end, someone could be terribly hurt."

"And you are worried that it will be you and mother, Papa?" Chrysis asked.

"I am worried that it will be any of us, my daughter. Or all of us."

4

Chrysis returned to Paris in early September, while her parents stayed on longer in Brittany. She and Bogey had corresponded almost daily while she was away, yet both wondered if this long separation would dull their passion for each other. She arrived at the Gare Montparnasse on a late train, and walked to her family's apartment on the blvd. Edgar-Quinet, where she telephoned her parents. Then she left again and walked the short distance around the corner to Bogey's flat to which she had a key. He did not know she was coming home on that day, and she had decided to wait for him there and surprise him when he returned from work. She fell asleep on his bed, waking only when she heard his key turning in the lock.

He came to her and sat on the edge of the bed. He smiled. "I caught your scent before I even opened the door," he said, "and I knew that you were home."

"Do you still love me?"

"No, I forgot all about you during these past six weeks."

"That's not funny."

"Nor true," Bogey said with a gentle smile. "Of course I still love you, more than ever. I felt as if some essential piece of me was missing while you were gone—something you had given back to me, and in your absence had taken away again."

"That's exactly how I felt," she said. "I went out painting with father nearly every day, but without you the results of my work lacked life."

"Maybe that's because you were so far from the bordellos and nightclubs you so love."

"Well, that, too, of course!" she said, and they laughed. "However, I did manage to find a couple of working girls who were...shall we say, "taking care" of the sailors in port, and, independent of father, I made one worthwhile painting of them in a room overlooking the sea."

"But of course you did," Bogey said.

"I call it *The Fortune Teller* and I think it is rather lively."

Chrysis sat up then and put her arms around Bogey, and they held each other tightly, both feeling complete again. And then they undressed as quickly as they could and made love with all the sweet passion of reunion, a kind of mutual urgency that demanded immediate satisfaction, and when Bogey entered her they became one being again. Afterwards, they lay together and talked until dawn, and finally they slept in each other's arms, their bodies so perfectly fitted one to the other that when Chrysis woke briefly to the sun, she imagined that their entwined sleeping forms were the work of a master sculptor.

5

They lived those next months within the rarefied cocoon of their love, a place with an atmosphere and climate quite distinct from that in which everyone else in Paris existed, or so it always seems to young lovers. Although happier than either of them had ever been, they shared the unspoken sense that they had created this space as a kind of shield to protect something rare that could not survive in the real world, in the same way that only the greenhouse allows a tropical orchid to thrive in northern climes.

Chrysis once again resumed her classes with Professor Humbert, and in January of 1928 she turned 21 years old. Although it was only an arbitrary number, and she had felt like an adult long prior to that, the birthday did allow her a certain further independence from her parents. Despite the fact that she was still living under their roof, she felt freer to come and go at whatever hours she wished, without explanation of where she had been or where she was going. And often, if she was very late and worried about waking them, she would simply sleep in the daybed in her atelier. Nor did she any longer feel that she needed her father's approval of the outfits she chose to wear. Rather she continued to explore her own eclectic sense of style and offbeat shopping sources, always pushing the limits of fashion, as she pushed every limit.

One spring evening before Bogey picked her up for dinner and a night of dancing, she came into her parents' salon dressed in a straight shift dress made from orange silk embroidered with Egyptian motifs, split up one side all the way to her thigh. With this she wore ankle-strap heel shoes, and around her neck a varied selection of colored African beads from choker to waist length, her hair done up in twisted lace braids.

"Yet another costume ball, my daughter?" said the colonel. "Let me guess…Cleopatra? An African princess? A Nubian slave girl dressed for sacrifice to the pagan gods?"

"Colonel…" warned Chrysis's mother.

"No, Papa, we are simply going dancing tonight."

"Will you not catch a chill with so much of your leg exposed?" he asked.

"The purpose of that, my father," Chrysis answered, "in addition, of course to titillation, is for freedom of movement on the dance floor."

"In that case, why wear anything at all?" the colonel asked.

"Believe me, in some of the clubs we have frequented, I have seen women thus on the dance floor from time to time.

The colonel could only shake his head at this insane new world that seemed to have completely usurped the one in which he had grown up.

"Well, I think you look absolutely stunning, my dear," said her mother admiringly. "How I wish that my generation of women had known one-tenth the freedom of yours. I have been asking your father to take me out to one of the neighborhood jazz clubs, but he believes that kind of dancing is effeminate and undignified for a military man."

"Bogey is a military man, Papa," Chrysis said, "as well as a wonderful dancer, whom no one has ever accused of being effeminate. If you'd like, I could teach you a few steps of the *Charleston* or the *Lindy Hop*, and you and mother could practice here at home.

The two women looked at each other conspiratorially, and they began to giggle at the image of the colonel performing the popular dance steps of the day, and soon they had dissolved into uncontrollable laughter until they were weeping. Accustomed to being the minority male in the household, the colonel was not without a certain dry sense of humor, even at his own expense. He had to admit the comedic potential of him dancing the *Lindy Hop,* and beneath his disapproving scowl, broke a small, sly smile.

CHRYSIS & BOGEY

1928 - 1929

1

Another summer came and went, and one mild autumn evening in early September, while Chrysis and Bogey were having an aperitif on the terrace of La Closerie des Lilas, she suddenly took his hand in hers. “Darling, have you ever been to an orgy?” she asked.

Bogey laughed. “About the closest I came was when I was living in the whorehouse in New York, and I sometimes slept with two or three of the girls at a time.”

“Ah, yes, your apprenticeship with the professionals!” Chrysis said, laughing, too. “After which you were awarded your diploma as master lovemaker!”

“And you, sweetheart?” he asked. “Have you ever been to an orgy?”

“Once. Casmir took me. It was in the spring of the year after I first saw you in Le Select.”

“And how was it?”

“Intense, nearly overwhelming,” Chrysis answered, “to the point that I’m not sure I would ever wish to do it again. There was almost too much sensory stimuli to bear. For a moment I felt like I was going to pass out.”

“What made you ask me that question?”

“Because I have an idea for a painting of an orgy,” she said. “And if I can get it done in time, I want to present the piece to the selection committee for the January exhibition at the Salon des Indépendants. Pascin has offered to submit some of my work for consideration.

I already have a clear image of the painting in my mind. However, it will require that I organize my own orgy. Will you help me, Bogey?"

Bogey laughed again. "You know, I have to tell you that you are the very first girl who has ever asked me to help her organize an orgy," he said. "And yet, why am I not surprised?"

"Because you know me too well," she said. "But perhaps this will surprise you: I want us both to participate in the orgy. Would you do that for me?"

"Ok, I admit it, this time you *have* surprised me." Bogey considered the question for some time. Accustomed to her lover's long silences and thoughtful deliberations, Chrysis waited patiently for his answer.

"Alright," he said finally. "Yes, I will do anything for you, sweetheart, anything you ask of me, and anything for the sake of your art. But does this mean I must have sex with men? Because that's an activity which has never held any interest to me."

"You do not have to have sex with anyone if you don't want to," she said. "...well, except, of course, with me."

"That part will be easy," he said. "But how can you participate in the orgy and paint it the same time?"

"I will add myself later," she said. "I have it all worked out. You see, I have this theory that in order to make a true representation of something, beyond the technical skill required, one must also have an intimate knowledge of the subject matter. Better yet one must experience it. Do you not find this to be true of the stories you write?"

"Of course, but then I only write true stories about things I know and have experienced," Bogey said. "Which is why I do not consider myself to be a real writer. I don't know how to make things up, I just tell what happens. So how can I help you with your orgy?"

"With the guest list. I want it to be friends, or friends of friends, people we know and trust who will be relaxed with each other, people who will have fun together. I want to remove the pornographic stigma from the idea of the orgy. I want it to be sensual, erotic and fun all at the same time. And I want different nationalities and races represented. Of course, I'm going to invite Juliette. And my two best friends from the atelier whom you have met—the Berliner, Marika, and the girl from Guadalajara, Rosario, rather free spirits both of them. That will give me a redhead, a blond, and a brunette—a French, a German, and a Mexican. And I'm going to invite Casmir, and of course you, darling—a Polish gypsy poet and an American cowboy/soldier/writer/boxer/gunslinger. I'd like for you to invite Jerome, and ask him to bring his little androgynous friend, Misha, from the *Ballet Russe.* Then I would have a homosexual American Indian painter, and a bisexual Russian dancer. And, to be sure, we must have food, wine and champagne. And music, I want music and laughter to be in the painting, as well as love and desire...and perhaps a little mystery. I'd also like for you to invite the piano player, Benny, from La Belle Poule. And I'll invite the Martiniquais string man, Yanis, from the band at Le Bal Nègre. In addition to being a fine musician, he has the largest, most joyful smile I have ever seen."

"I can see that you have already given this event a great deal of consideration," Bogey said, "and are assembling a truly international cast of characters, of all colors and persuasions."

"Exactly the point," Chrysis said. "And all of us in the arts in one way or another. You see, I want this painting to represent the village itself, to serve as a kind of metaphor for these times in Montparnasse."

"Juliette? In the arts?"

"An artist of sex. There is no denying that, is there? But we must hurry as the deadline for submissions to the Salon is fast approaching. I will need to allow myself time to execute the painting and to let it dry before I can present it."

2

And thus preparations were made, guests confirmed, a date and time set. Chysis had decided to hold the bacchanalia in her atelier on the blvd. Edgar-Quinet when she knew that her parents would be at their home in the country for an extended stay. She expected that the orgy would last at least over the course of a full 24-hours, and she arranged with Madame Mireille for Juliette, Bogey, and the piano player, Benny, to all have a rare Saturday night off from work. Her plan was to make a number of different sketches during the duration of the affair for later reference. As a number of other artists had ateliers in the building, and were frequently up to their own late-hour mischief, Chrysis assumed that no one would complain to her parents upon their return, in case matters got out of hand, which they seemed almost certain to do.

Bogey arrived early on the appointed day, as she had asked him to. They were both oddly nervous in the reality of the moment, entering as they were new territory in their relationship, which had until now, not only been sexually monogamous, but also largely confined to the two of them, shutting out the rest of the world within their lover's cocoon. At the same time, they both felt an exciting element of inchoate danger in the prospect of walking together into this unknown land.

"Nothing that happens here this weekend," Chrysis said now, "must be allowed to interfere with our love. That is something sacred."

"Agreed," Bogey answered.

"At the same time," she added, "nothing that might interfere with our love, must be allowed to happen. Our primary responsibility is to be respectful of one another."

"You know more about this than I, Chrysis," Bogey said, "but it seems to me that trying to assume responsibility and control over what happens in an orgy is counter to the entire spirit of the event."

"You are right, of course," she said. "I am just afraid of going too far and of breaking what we have together. I could not bear that."

"Let us just say then that our only responsibility is to your painting, and for you to be free to do the work you need to do. For my part, I can promise you, nothing that happens here this weekend will change my feelings toward you. I have no idea what to expect, but I am ready for anything, and everything."

"Thank you, my love, that makes me feel much better."

In this same spirit of anticipation, both excited and apprehensive, the other guests began to arrive. To create the correct ambiance, Chrysis had closed all the shutters in the atelier, in the same way that they were kept perpetually closed at La Belle Poule; champagne bottles had been opened and placed on ice, and candles lit to help everyone settle into the right sensual mood. So that she could capture different angles of the activities, she had set up three separate easels in the room, illuminated themselves by just enough candlelight for her to be able to sketch and paint behind them.

Chrysis was grateful to have Juliette present, for in addition to being an intimate friend, she had the most experience in such matters, and her easy humor and good-nature helped to put everyone else at ease.

"My goodness, such a handsome redskin!" Juliette said to Jerome, who at Chrysis's urging had brought his family's ceremonial headdress for the occasion. "I have never made love to a real Indian before. Although I do have a client who likes to dress up like one."

"That doesn't count," Jerome said. "It has been my experience that many French people have American Indian fetishes. I am always amused each year during the *Le Bal des Quat'z'Arts* by all the students who dress as Indians. It reminds me of Al Jolson in black face."

"That is because we French honor your race," Juliette said. "As we honor that of the Negro."

"I must tell you honestly, mademoiselle, that you will still not have the opportunity to make love to a real Indian," said Jerome, as he patted the butt of his companion, Misha. "For this brave prefers boys."

"Ah, we shall just see about that, big Chief," said Juliette, cupping Jerome's cheek affectionately in her hand, "Anything can happen at a good orgy, and that is all part of the fun."

The German girl, Marika, was initially the most shy of the group, but Casmir quickly took charge of her and relaxed her with his seductive gypsy poet sensibilities. In contrast, Rosario was immediately in the spirit of the event. The daughter of a prominent Spanish land grant family, who owned vast ranches in the states of

Chihuahua and Sonora, as well as a palatial home in Mexico City, she was a small, trim, lively girl, who wore her dark hair bobbed in the style of the *quartier*. She, too, painted in the bold expressionist colors and form that Chrysis admired. The two of them had become friendly at the atelier, because, of all the students, they most pushed the limits of Professor Humbert's authority.

Yanis, the Martiniquais string man, had brought his banjo, while Benny sat at Chrysis's mother's piano. They began playing the latest jazz tunes, and as the champagne and music took their desired effects, all began to dance. Misha, lithe and graceful as only a ballet dancer can be, had changed into a grass skirt for the event, with grass anklets and sandals, a kind of white male version of Josephine Baker, and he made everyone laugh appreciatively with his great leaps and pirouettes to the strains of the hit song from America, *Uncanny Banjo.* Between them, Benny and Yanis knew a vast repertoire of songs, both slow and fast, jazz and blues, and they both had fine singing voices.

Music, dancing and champagne in the soft candlelight, laughter and gaiety, and soon the guests were holding each other and kissing affectionately, like old friends and lovers, shedding inhibitions with various articles of clothing. Chrysis moved between her easels, the song and dance finding their way into her brushes. Juliette wore a semi-transparent black dress, slit up the leg and trimmed with fringe, and as Yanis began to play the new Cole Porter song, *Let's Do it, Let's Fall in Love,* she asked Bogey to dance with her. She held him close and he felt her body through the thin fabric, tight against his own, the inevitable stirrings of the flesh.

"You and I share much in common," she whispered.

"Yes, I know, so Chrysis has told me."

"I have never had the opportunity to correctly thank you for what you did when Maurice came looking for me that night," she said. "I would have done so, but as you know, Madame Mireille is rather strict about the girls fraternizing with the staff."

"There is no need for you to thank me," Bogey said.

"But I want to. You saved my life. Perhaps as the night progresses, I will have the opportunity to display my eternal gratitude."

Casmir danced with Marika, whispering erotic poetry in her ear. Yanis took a break from the banjo, removed his white shirt, damp from his exertions, revealing his broad dark upper body, upon which the candlelight flickered as if in a mirror. When he cut in on Casmir for a dance with the blond, who had never before danced with a black man, the poet did not protest, but danced instead with Rosario, and then with Misha. The dancer wore red lipstick upon his full-lipped mouth, and could easily have passed for a young girl, so that when he unexpectedly kissed the gypsy, who was a sensually sophisticated fellow, Casmir did not resist but kissed the boy back. This made Jerome jealous and the Cheyenne then danced with little Rosario, who had a slim, boyish, small-breasted figure herself, and when he kissed her, hoping to make Misha jealous in turn, he had to admit that he rather liked the feel of the Mexican's lips on his, her slender body in his arms. Misha laughed. In this way the barriers, taboos and prejudices, the races, nationalities, and sexes gradually fell away in the course of the evening—black, white, Indian, Mexican, Pole, German, French, American, Martiniquais, heterosexual, homosexual, bisexual, men, women, androgynous—this great melting pot Chrysis had so carefully assembled, all merging as if indistinguishable in the dreamlike spirit of the night. They danced and they drank and they smoked, they sang and they laughed and they made love. They ate and they talked and they slept. They woke to change partners and make love again. It was just as libertine, free, sensual, and joyful as Chrysis had envisioned it might be. She joined them periodically, and then returned to her easels and her various studies, to join them again later. With the shutters closed tight, it was impossible to know the hour, or how much time had passed, and no one cared or wished to know and eventually all slept again in various postures and embraces, and as they woke, one by one, they dressed quietly in their street clothes, and with only the slightest whispers of goodbye they each took their leave until the last guest had departed, and then it was over and only Bogey and Chrysis remained.

"We are OK, the two of us, aren't we, my love?" she asked him. "We survived this intact, did we not?"

"Yes, sweetheart, we did," Bogey answered. "We are just fine."

3

Over the next two weeks, Chrysis worked virtually nonstop on the painting, *Orgie*, hardly sleeping, eating, or bathing. As her various sketches coalesced into the final canvas, it was as if she was reliving the entire experience, and she painted with the same kind of erotic energy and passion as the orgy itself, falling asleep for an hour or two, curled on the mats on the floor of her atelier or on the daybed, waking to light a cigarette, drink a cup of coffee, and work again. Now and then when she remembered to, she ate a piece of cheese or sausage and stale baguette, and drank a glass of wine. She did not see Bogey during this time, and he left her alone, knowing well that when she was ready she would come to him.

One afternoon, she knocked on his door, and when Bogey opened it she threw her arms around him. Her long thick hair was loose and wild around her face, splattered with paint, and she smelled of oil, pigments, turpentine and cigarettes, with an undercurrent of her own body odor.

"You look and smell like you've been to a long, long orgy...with paint," Bogey teased.

"That is exactly where I've been, and what I've been doing," she said. "I'm sorry, I just had to come see you right away. I'm a mess, I know, and I stink. But I had to see you....I finished the painting..."

They held each other tightly, and they both had the sense of having come home in each other's arms, the comforting solace of intimacy. "I like the way you look, and smell," Bogey said. "I've missed you. Congratulations, darling." He took her to his bed, and as soon as he entered her she came violently as if all the relived passions of the past two weeks, as well as those of all the characters in the painting had suddenly exploded inside her.

Chrysis slept for fourteen hours and when she woke she asked Bogey if he would take a walk with her in the Luxembourg Gardens. She had hardly been outside in the past two weeks, and needed some fresh air and exercise. It was a magnificent October day, clear and crisp. She wore her paint-splotched farmer's coat, her hands, hair and face still brightly speckled with oil paint, which glistened in the early morning sunlight, so that she seemed a kind of riotous, unkempt extension of the garden itself, a wild palette of colors that complemented the changing leaves on the trees, and the autumnal flowers in their final burst of bloom.

"Are you going to show me the painting?" Bogey asked.

"No, I want everyone to see it for the first time in a real exhibition," she answered. "You, the other models, my parents, Professor Humbert…everyone. I have no idea how people will react, although I have a fair sense of what father's opinion will be…but you see, in this way I will be a little protected, insulated, surrounded by friends, colleagues, the public, and the other artists present."

Bogey could hardly protest, for he had still never let Chrysis, nor anyone else, read any of his stories. "I understand," he said. "But what if it is not accepted by the Salon?"

"It will be."

Two weeks later, after the painting had dried sufficiently to transport, Chrysis took *Orgie* to Pascin's studio on the blvd. Clichy, with two other pieces she wished to submit for consideration to the Salon des Indépendants. Although he was working, the painter welcomed her graciously, shooing away his two half-dressed models, who wore the grey slips he preferred them to pose in. Pascin had been particularly friendly toward both Chrysis and Bogey ever since the incident with Maurice Toscan, which he liked to refer to dramatically as: *"Gunfight at La Belle Poule: Cowboy Versus Gangsters."*

Chrysis unwrapped the two smaller canvases first, which Pascin placed on chairs, and then *Orgie,* which he set up on an easel, taking several steps back to have a look at all three together. She could feel the steady drumbeat of her heart against her chest as Pascin studied the paintings for what seemed like an eternity. Finally, he nodded. "Alright, now I see that you really do have talent, and that, indeed, you do model for yourself," he said. "We have very different styles, you and I, but, clearly, similar interests. However, I must admit, your work is riskier than mine. You paint boldly, with exuberance and frankness, which are not qualities that can be taught in the ateliers. I will make an appointment this week with the director of the Salon, and together we will take these paintings to show him."

4

The leaves on the trees of Paris turned brown and fluttered to the ground, and the soft weather of autumn gave way to the cold and damp of winter. The holidays rushed by and on Friday, January 18, five days before Chrysis's 22nd birthday, the Salon des Indépendants, 1929, opened with two of her paintings hanging in the Grand Palais. One was *Orgie* and the other, less controversial, entitled *Shadows & Lights*, a Parisian street scene that reflected a certain foreboding Chrysis had been feeling all through the dying season and on into the New Year.

The Salon was to be Chrysis's first professional exhibition, and, of course, her parents would be attending the opening, along with several of her friends from the atelier and others from the neighborhood. She had also invited Pascin, Soutine, and Kisling, Madame Mireille and her husband Père Jean, and all those who had modeled for *Orgie*. And, to be sure, Professor Jacques Ferdnand Humbert.

The professor was shortly to celebrate his 87th birthday, and at the beginning of the semester had announced to the class that this would be his final year of teaching the atelier, over which he had now presided for a full 29 years. Despite whatever differences the two may have had, Chrysis felt privileged to have studied under Humbert at the end of his distinguished career, and she was pleased to be able to honor him before his retirement by finally having her work accepted by one of the major salons. At least she hoped he would consider it an honor, for like all artists, she was inevitably nervous about the reception of her paintings, particularly by the two major authority figures in her life—her teacher and her father.

Other than Pascin, no one else had yet viewed *Orgie*, but as Chrysis had anticipated, there was some comfort in being surrounded by the other artists at this year's exhibition. As requested by the organizers, they had all arrived early at the Grand Palais, giving them time to circulate and admire each other's work. There were over 500 paintings in that year's exhibition, and, to be sure, it would be impossible to see them all on this first night.

Chrysis's mother had taken her shopping for an outfit to wear to the event, and she was dressed in an exquisite dark silk jacquard, dolman-sleeved dress in a floral pattern, yoke and cuffs overlaid with gold crocheted detail, teamed with a lamé wrap in a large stencil print with sage russed-velvet on the cuffs and around the neck. On her feet, she wore silk pumps with crisscross ribbons around her ankles, and around her neck a large oriental-theme brooch on a velvet choker, while a cacophony of bangles adorned her wrists. She wore mascara on her large deep-set eyes, and her full lips were painted Chinese red. The full effect of all this was quite a transformation from Chrysis's daily work clothes, or the bohemian outfits she sported about the neighborhood. She was a graceful, elegant young woman in full bloom.

Bogey arrived with Jerome and Misha, and Juliette with Madame Mireille and Père Jean. Casmir had been seeing Marika these past months, and they, too, came to the Palais together, as did the musicians Benny and Yanis. Rosario arrived alone. Chrysis had asked them all to meet her in the lobby. It was the first time the orgy participants had been reunited since the event itself nearly four months earlier, and initially they were oddly shy and tongue-tied in each others' presence. Chrysis escorted the group en masse into the salon and led them directly to *Orgie.*

Variously dressed for the affair in their most formal attire, they stood at first silently before the painting, feeling suddenly naked in the face of the artist's representation, with the realization that all of the people coming to the exhibition tonight, and for as long as this painting survived, were going to view them thus. Indeed, they all had the same strange sensation that they needed to check to make sure they were wearing their clothes. But then all at once they broke into laughter, and began chatting animatedly, teasing one another and joking, remembering both the gaiety and the eroticism of the scene portrayed, and falling back into the same comfortable intimacy.

"Juliette!" said Jerome, "Look, you are the star of the painting!"

"As I was the star of the orgy!" she answered. "But Chief, you look so serious!"

"Can't you see?" Jerome said. "Chrysis has captured my jealousy that my little Misha is regarding you with such lust."

"You know," said Casmir, gazing thoughtfully at the canvas, "some day many years in the future, when there is nothing left of any of us but dust and ash, people of a distant generation may look at this painting and wonder about us; they will wonder who all these crazy people are having such fun in Paris in the autumn of 1928."

Bogey was dressed in his black cowboy suit and string tie, with black dress boots, and his large, shiny silver rodeo buckle on his belt, an outfit his mother had sent to him, believing that he needed correct clothing for a sophisticated city like Paris, which she had only seen in the encyclopedia and in magazines at the county library, and would never see in person. Chrysis came to him now, took him by the arm and led him a bit away from the group. "How handsome you look tonight, my love," she said.

"And you…how beautiful you are, sweetheart," he answered. "More beautiful than ever."

"I want you to tell me what you see about us in the painting?" she asked.

Bogey looked again at *Orgie* for a long moment before answering. "I see that we are a little apart from the others," he said, "on the very edge of the canvas, as if we are about to fall off it altogether. I see from the way we are looking at each other how much in love we are, how much we desire each other, and that despite the presence of the others, we are in our own private world where we have always lived together."

"Yes, that's right," she said, "that's what I was trying to portray. In addition to everything else, I wanted this to be a kind of homage to our love, which seems an odd thing to say about a painting of an orgy. But you see that, don't you? You see it all. I cannot tell you how happy that makes me."

"There is one thing that I'm not entirely clear about," Bogey said.

"And what is that, my love?"

"Except for your red lips, and the skin tone and flush of passion on your face, you have painted yourself without color, as a gray figure. Why?"

"I am not exactly sure," Chrysis answered. "Perhaps because that color red, that flush of passion as you put it, is what best defines me, and my body needed no further color. Or perhaps it is just so that I, as the artist, remain a little unfinished, a work still in progress."

It was then that Chrysis turned and saw her father, mother, and Professor Humbert walking toward them. As they approached, the others instinctively sensed their friend's anxiety, and began to drift off one by one, to browse among the other work hanging in the salon, as if the collective force of the colonel's and the professor's presence was driving them away. Only Bogey remained standing there.

"I think it might be best if you circulated a bit, too, my love," Chrysis said to him. "I should probably do this alone."

Bogey nodded. He greeted the Jungbluths, and Chrysis introduced him to Professor Humbert, and then he excused himself.

Her father, mother, and the professor now studied the painting, the vast salon suddenly shrinking down to this single intimate familial scene, all other guests disappearing as if the four of them were alone in the room, and the only sound in the artist's ears was the metronome beating of her own heart.

Finally, her mother spoke first: "It is quite…how shall I say?...quite *energetic*, my dear. Yes, that is the word, energetic, indeed."

"Thank you, Mother."

And now it was Professor Humbert's turn to weigh in: "With all the paintings hanging here today," he said, "yours was the very first I noticed when I entered the salon—perhaps partly because you are my student and I am familiar with your palette. But also because it draws ones eyes. It has power and luminosity. It is vibrant, colorful, and frank. And your forms are largely correct. Well done, young lady, I am proud of you."

In the four years that Chrysis had studied under Professor Humbert, this was by far the highest praise he had ever bestowed upon her, and she blushed deeply, and fought back the tears she had controlled so well whenever the professor had savaged her work in one of his tirades during class.

And now, lastly, the colonel spoke. "As a trusting father," he said, his voice tight and cool, "I can only assume that this is not how my daughter spends her time when her parents are away from the city. And so I, too, congratulate you for your exceptionally vivid imagination." Colonel Jungbluth turned to his wife. "My dear, let us view some of the other fine work hanging here this evening." Marie-Reine took her husband's arm, looked at her daughter with that familiar glance of resignation between them, and the Jungbluths moved on.

"Well, looking on the bright side," said Chrysis to the professor, as she watched them go. "I suppose that my father's reaction could have been worse."

"Mademoiselle Jungbluth," said Professor Humbert, "it is not the purview of either the critic or the viewer of art to judge a painting based upon the personal life of the artist, or vice-versa, to judge the personal life of the artist, based upon their work. However, I'm afraid that it *is* the privilege of the parent to do so. As art, your painting stands on its own merits. As a family matter…well, as a family matter, that is another question, is it not?"

"Thank you, Professor," Chrysis said with a grateful smile, "you have been very kind to me tonight. Regardless of any differences we may have had over these past years, I want you to know that it has been my great honor to be your student. Thank you. I will never forget the debt I owe you, and I hope you will forgive me for any insolence I may have displayed toward you."

"My dear Chrysis," said the professor, addressing her by her first name for the first time since they had known each other, "I can assure you that in the course of my long career, you are not the first headstrong student I have encountered. Indeed, the best artists I have instructed over the years, have usually been the most difficult."

"I accept that as a great compliment, Professor."

5

Chrysis was kept occupied for the remainder of the evening with visitors to the exhibition. Pascin came by with his paramour Lucy Krogh, to say hello and to congratulate her, as did Soutine accompanied by Paulette Jourdain. It would be a night of beginnings and endings for Chrysis—her first professional exhibition, and the first real sale of her career, for on that opening night she sold *Orgie* to a collector for 7000 French francs. Of course, before the new owner was able to take it home, it would hang until the exhibition ended on February 28. She was pleased and proud to have sold the painting, and felt a certain sense of validation. But after it was tagged with the sale marker, she felt, too, a strange sadness and emptiness, to think that after all that planning and work, this very personal piece would now hang in the home of strangers, never to be seen by her again.

And as to other endings, although Chrysis could not know this, and never would know the full truth, while she was thus preoccupied with the business of art, Colonel Jungbluth approached Bogey in another room of the Salon and asked to speak with him privately. Bogey followed the colonel to the vestibule, where they retrieved their hats and overcoats, and stepped outside. It was cold, but clear. They both lit cigarettes.

"Bogart, I realize that you were greatly affected by your experiences in the war," the colonel began. "I have known stronger men than you who were broken by those terrible years—fine soldiers who descended into alcoholism, drug use, perversion and madness."

"Yes sir," said Bogey, uneasily, wondering where this conversation was headed.

"Since my daughter met you, and brought you to our home," continued the colonel, "I have always considered you to be an upstanding young man, practically like a son to me. However, I have been disturbed by the fact that after all these years in Europe, you have made no effort to return to your own family, to your own country."

The colonel took a long drag on his cigarette. "I know my daughter," he said on the exhale. "I believe that I know her better than anyone in the world—better than you, better even than her mother. I have long since acknowledged and accepted the fact that she possesses an adventurous, rebellious side. At the same time, I know that she is a good girl, a sensible girl, a well-brought up girl. Having seen that painting tonight, I recognize that only the most insidious influences of an older man, and a very troubled man, could possibly lead her to descend into that deviant world.

Bogey began to speak up in his own defense, but the colonel waved his words away with the hand in which he held his cigarette. "Yes, yes, of course," he continued, "she changed certain features of the characters portrayed, but believe me, I had no difficulty identifying the two of you. And I understand now how foolish I have been about you, young man, how blind I have been. This evening, when I first saw you in the company of your degenerate friends, it became ever clearer to me how seriously I have misjudged your character. I will not have you corrupt my daughter, my only child, any further than you already have. Do I make myself clear, Bogart?"

"Not entirely," Bogey said. "What is it that you want from me, Colonel Jungbluth?"

"I want you to leave Paris. I want you to return to America—and without my daughter."

"With all due respect, sir," said Bogey, "your daughter is about to turn 22 years old. As an adult she is free to make her own decisions about her future."

"And what do you expect that future to be?" the colonel asked. "Do you imagine that she is going to return to the United States with you? To a tiny ranching community in northern Colorado? What would she do there? Give up her art career? Teach in a one-room schoolhouse like your mother? Raise a brood of little cowboys? Or perhaps you plan to stay here in Paris working for the rest of your life as a barman in a brothel? Yes, I know many people in the neighborhood, young man, and I have been informed of your true place of employment, although you and my daughter deceived me about it.

"And if I refuse your request, Colonel?"

"Ah, well, apparently I have not yet made myself clear," said the colonel. "This is not a request I am making of you, Legionnaire Lambert. I am giving you a direct order. And if you choose to disobey it, then you will force me to inform the Foreign Legion, that, indeed, the cowboy courier did not die in the war, after all. Rather he fled to Scotland, where he lived anonymously for a number of years, before finally returning to France under a false passport. You see, such information would almost certainly result in a full inquiry by military tribunal, not to mention a great deal of press attention, all focused upon you, Bogart. Of course, I do not believe that you would be punished in any way. Quite the contrary—you would become a national celebrity, the returned hero, a kind of circus sideshow. At the very least, the anonymity you so cherish would be forever breached."

"And you would do that to me, would you, Colonel?"

Colonel Jungbluth looked hard at Bogey. "Only if you force me to."

"What if I simply tell Chrysis about this conversation?" Bogey asked. "That you are trying to coerce me into leaving her? What then, Colonel?"

"Then you would most likely destroy a loving relationship between a father and daughter," said the colonel. "I would hope that as a once-distinguished soldier, you might have sufficient honor left to avoid doing such a thing. Have you not already caused enough damage to my daughter by leading her into your world of perversion?"

The two men looked hard into each other's eyes for a long moment. Finally Bogey nodded. "It will take me some time to make the necessary arrangements to leave the country, Colonel," he said.

"Of course," said the colonel. "Take what time you need, Legionnaire Lambert. But be gone by spring."

6

Chrysis had so much energy pent up from the excitement of the opening, that upon the close of the evening's exhibition she asked Bogey if he would mind walking home with her rather than taking the metro.

"I sold both my paintings," she said, as they stepped outside the Grand Palais, their breath visible in the frigid January air.

"I saw that you did," Bogey answered. "Congratulations, sweetheart. You are a true professional now."

"I am, aren't I?" she said, "I hadn't even considered that yet. I am a professional painter, no longer just a student of art."

They crossed Le Pont Alexandra III to the Quai d'Orsay, and then to the blvd. Saint-Germain, walking fast against the cold, their long strides in perfect step, as always.

"I saw you leave the Salon earlier with father," Chrysis said.

"Yes, we went out for some fresh air and a smoke."

"Did he say anything to you about the painting?"

"We didn't really talk about that."

"I will have to face him about it tonight when I get home," she said. "Or more likely tomorrow."

"May I ask you something, Chrysis?" Bogey said.

"Of course, darling, but why are you being so serious? What's the matter?"

"If I asked you to marry me and come to America, would you?"

"Are you proposing to me?"

"No, not exactly, I'm just asking you a hypothetical question."

"Do you mean would I marry you now and go to America?" Chrysis asked. "Right now? But I still have another semester at the atelier with Professor Humbert."

"Alright then, let's say at the end of the semester," Bogey asked. "Would you go then, at the beginning of the summer. Or let's say even next year?"

"Did father talk to you about this tonight? Is that why you're asking me now?"

"No."

"I love you, Bogey," she said. "You know that. But I'm just getting started in my career. Soutine told me tonight that I could very likely exhibit in this year's Salon d'Automne. And in any case, what would I do in Colorado? How could I progress as an artist out there in the middle of nowhere? I would have to give up everything, wouldn't I? My family, my career, France. I barely even speak English."

"I understand, of course, I do," Bogey said. "I've known all that from the beginning; we both have. I just wanted to hear you say it."

"But you're not thinking of leaving, are you? Not now?"

"I have received a letter from my mother," he said. "My father is not well." Bogey's eyes filled with tears; he had never before lied to Chrysis, and it felt physically painful. "They need me back on the ranch. You know, I have been away now for almost twelve years. We have both always known that one day I would have to return."

"Oh, God, but why are you telling me this now?" Chrysis asked.

"Because I have only just today received the letter," he said. "I'm sorry, darling, I did not mean to ruin your triumphant evening."

"You have not ruined it, my love," she said. "There would be no good time for you to tell me this kind of news."

"I do not have to leave right away," Bogey said. "Not until the spring, so let's not worry about it just now. Let's not talk about it anymore. I'm sorry I even brought it up tonight. We should be celebrating your success. We're all dressed up, and it's early yet. Let's go dancing all night, and drink champagne."

7

Bogey purchased a third-class ticket for passage in April on the *S.S. Leviathon* from the port of Cherbourg to New York. He would still have to travel on the counterfeit British passport Archie Munro had secured for him, and he had no idea whether or not it would be accepted when he disembarked in America. But he would deal with that when the time came.

In those next few months together, Bogey and Chrysis were more deeply connected than ever. Against her parents' objections, she moved out of their apartment and into Bogey's, and they lived like a real couple. They did not discuss his impending departure, preferring to pretend with the blind faith of young love that all was as it had always been between them, and would always remain. And they kept alive the illusion that the separation was only temporary, that Bogey would be returning soon to France, and when the time was right at some undefined point in the future, they would marry, and Chrysis would move to America.

Spring came to Paris, the trees broke their buds and leafed out with the fresh, bright green of the new season, the promise of renewal. The flowers blossomed in the parks and gardens of the city, and the outdoor terraces of the cafés opened again and filled with pale citizens blinking in the unfamiliar sunlight. The bicyclists took to the streets, and young lovers walked arm in arm.

Bogey had quit his job at La Belle Poule and he and Chrysis went to the museums and the spring art exhibitions at the galleries, living like vacationing tourists, not wishing to miss anything, for who could say when they would be in Paris together again?

Two days before Bogey's ship sailed, they took the train to Cherbourg and checked into a small *pension* in the fisherman's wharf neighborhood on the edge of the city. They took their meals next door in a restaurant overlooking the wharf, where they ate the freshly caught seafood of the region. Only at their last dinner together, did they speak openly of his departure.

"How does it feel to be going home, my love?" Chrysis asked after the table had been cleared of dishes, and they were finishing their wine.

"It feels strange," Bogey answered. "These past few days I've had the feeling that I've forgotten something, like in one of those bad dreams, where you know you've forgotten something, and you're looking everywhere for it, but you can't quite remember what it is you've forgotten. Do you understand what I mean?"

"Yes."

"And then when I woke up this morning," Bogey said, "it suddenly hit me. I came over here all those years ago with my horse, and now I'm going home without him. That is what I forgot. I left Crazy Horse here in France. And now I am leaving you."

From her purse, Chrysis pulled a piece of rolled sketch paper tied in a silk ribbon. "I brought you a little going away present," she said, sliding it across the table to Bogey.

Bogey untied the ribbon, and unrolled the paper.

"I made that drawing when I was twelve years old," Chrysis said, "and my father told me the story about you and Crazy Horse. I've kept it all this time. I think my painting technique has improved since then, don't you?"

Bogey had picked up the drawing to study. At the top Chrysis had written in her childish scrawl, *"The Cowboy Courier and Crazy Horse."* He smiled. "No," he said, shaking his head, "no, I don't think so. I think this is among your finest work, an excellent representation. I will take good care of it, as I expect someday when you are a famous painter it will be worth a great deal of money."

And they laughed.

"Thank you, sweetheart," Bogey said. "Truly, this means a great deal to me, and I will always cherish it." Now he reached into the inside pocket of his suit coat and pulled out a rolled cylinder of notepaper sheets, tied similarly with a leather thong. "I brought you a going away gift, as well," he said, handing the cylinder to Chrysis. She untied the thong and unrolled the paper, flattening it on the table.

"That is the story I was writing in my notebook on that winter evening at Le Select," said Bogey. "The very first time we ever saw each other. I'd like for you to wait and read it after I've left tomorrow."

They made love that night with the sweet urgency of parting, and they slept wrapped in each other's arms as they always had, as if they were each one-half of a single being. They woke in the middle of the night and made love again, and a third time upon waking at dawn.

They rose and dressed silently, the sun not yet risen, both now with butterflies of apprehension in their stomachs at the looming reality of separation. Bogey went downstairs to settle the bill with the proprietor of the *pension,* and to arrange to have his steamer trunk delivered to the ship. Then they took their last walk around the wharf, where the fishermen were loading their boats at dawn for the day's outing.

"I've always been most comfortable in the company of those who work outdoors," Bogey said, as they watched the men. "The people who do the actual physical work of the world. Funny, isn't it, that I ended up in Paris as a bartender in a brothel—working inside with the shutters always drawn? If I knew how to swim, maybe I would just stay here and become a fisherman, instead of going home to be a cattleman."

Chrysis faced him now, gripped his arms tight in her hands and looked deep into his eyes. "Do that, Bogey," she said. "Please, do that. I can teach you how to swim."

He cupped her cheek tenderly in his hand, and smiled. "I wish I could, sweetheart," he said. "Believe me, I wish I could."

Bogey opened the leather carpet bag he carried that contained all the modest items he needed for his passage across the sea. From it he pulled a small camera. "Jerome gave me this as a going-away gift," he said. "I didn't want to hurt his feelings by telling him that I'm not really interested in photography. But it occurs to me that I don't have a single photo of you to take home. There's enough light now. Walk out there on the dock a little way, and turn to face me. And smile, I want to remember you smiling."

And so Chrysis did as Bogey asked, and struck a pose on the dock and he took her photo. Then in anxious silence once again, they made the long walk to the main port where the large ships docked, and when they reached the berth of the *S.S. Leviathon,* passengers were already beginning to board.

Chrysis handed Bogey her tin of Craven "A" cigarettes. "Take these with you," she said. "And that way I can imagine you standing alone on the deck at night, looking out at the sea, smoking and thinking of me."

Bogey took her in his arms and held her tightly, and she held him tightly back. He felt her breasts against his chest, the swell of her sex against his, and she felt his chest against her breasts, the bulge of his sex against hers, both with the familiar sense, again and for the last time, that they were one together.

"I will come back for you," Bogey whispered in her ear. "One day I will come back for you. You know that, don't you, darling?"

"Yes," Chrysis whispered. "I know that, my love."

Epilogue

In memoriam

Gabrielle Odile Rosalie "Chrysis" JUNGBLUTH
Boulogne-sur-Mer, January 23, 1907 - Trinité, Martinique, May 3, 1989

Bogart Lambert never returned to France. In late October of 1929, on the final day of Chrysis Jungbluth's first exhibition at the Salon d'Automne in Paris, the New York stock market collapsed, precipitating the beginning of the long Great Depression, which would spread worldwide. The local bank in North Park, Colorado failed, and Bogey's family lost what little savings they had, and very nearly lost their ranch. But thanks largely to the return of their son, the Lamberts managed to hang on through those difficult years.

Jules Pascin hanged himself in his atelier in June of 1930, roughly punctuating the end of *les années folles* (the crazy years) of Montparnasse, in the same way that Modigliani's death had unofficially begun the decade in 1920. Chrysis joined the thousands of mourners—many of them waiters and barmen of the neighborhood establishments Pascin had so generously frequented during his lifetime—who walked behind the artist's coffin as it was transported from his studio on the blvd. Clichy to the Cemetery of Saint-Ouen.

Bogey and Chrysis corresponded regularly for well over a year after his departure, and then, as these things do, the frequency of their letters gradually tapered off, until finally ceasing altogether. Chrysis did much of the most sensual and finest work of her career in those early years, 1928-1932. In 1931, she became engaged to a promising young architect in Paris, an alliance largely arranged between their parents. Colonel Jungbluth proudly described his future son-in-law in a letter to an aunt in La Vendée, as a *"a tall and handsome boy, and a very hard worker."* However, several months before the planned wedding date, Chrysis broke off the engagement. She had come to the inevitable conclusion that she did not have the requisite fire in her loins for this boy, who, finally, was simply too conventional for her. In any case, when the time came, she preferred to choose her own husband rather than have her father do so.

By 1935, Chrysis, now 28-years old, remained still unwed, much to the distress of Colonel Jungbluth, who wrote the same aunt: *"My daughter is not yet married; it is very difficult today—there has been so much economic chaos, and so few young men who are not suffering from the crisis. It takes too much money to live, thus on both sides, everyone is being cautious, and the opportunities to make a good marriage are increasingly rare."*

One night in 1936, while dancing at Le Bal Nègre, Chrysis met a young medical student from Martinique named Roland Narfin. Five years her junior, Roland was a tall, handsome, charismatic fellow, and a marvelous dancer, and Chrysis asked him to come to her studio the next day so that she could paint a portrait of him.

Roland and Chrysis fell in love, and on August 18, 1938, they were married in a civil ceremony at City Hall by M. Emile Rothschild, the deputy mayor of the 14th arrondisement. Chrysis's mother, Marie-Reine, served as one of the witnesses, but Colonel Jungbluth himself was conspicuously absent from the wedding ceremony. One can well imagine how the colonel must have felt about his daughter marrying a black man from Martinique.

Roland Narfin graduated from medical school and became a physician in the French army. He and Chrysis stayed in France during the terrible years of World War II, and they lived primarily in Paris throughout the occupation. Because Roland cared for wounded soldiers, the Nazis had given him a pass that allowed him to come and go relatively freely.

Colonel Jungbluth and his wife had moved to the home of family members in Rocheservière, La Vendée before the outbreak of the war. Although thirteen years her husband's junior, Antoinette Augustine Marie-Reine Gatty Jungbluth, died of cancer on March 21, 1940 at 61 years of age.

After her mother's death, Chrysis spent as much time as she could with her father in La Vendée, while Roland was away treating the wounded in various field hospitals and clinics. Colonel Charles Ismaël Jungbluth—Commissioned Officer of Staff, Commander of the Legion of Honor, awarded the *Croix de Guerre,* eight citations for bravery—died of a heart attack in La Vendée on September 13, 1943 at age 76.

Throughout the 1930's and into the early war years, and again immediately afterwards, Chrysis Jungbluth continued to show her work in the major salons of Paris and in private exhibitions. In 1948, she and Roland left

France and moved to the island of Martinique, where he would practice medicine, and they would live for much of the rest of their married life. Chrysis kept an atelier on the rue Boissonade in Paris until the early 1970's, and she made occasional trips back to France during those intervening decades to visit family members in La Vendée. However, with the move to Martinique, which hardly had a vibrant international art community in the 1940s, 50s, and 60s, she largely sacrificed her career for life with Roland, and she was virtually forgotten by the Paris art world.

Chrysis continued to paint during her years in Martinique, and she was frequently seen around the island sketching scenes of native life. Her palette had completely changed in the Caribbean, but at the same time, her work had lost its youthful passion. Nevertheless, she had no great regrets at having given up her art career, for she and Roland were very happy, and they lived a grand love affair together for half a century.

Chrysis Jungbluth died at the couple's home in Martinique on May 3, 1989, at age 82. It was said by guests present at her burial that when the stone lid of her tomb fell closed with the definitive echo of forever, her husband Roland uttered a terrible, heartbroken cry of grief.

Upon his return to Colorado, Bogart Lambert discovered that after he had been reported missing in action and presumed dead in France, his old legionnaire friend, Fred Dunn, from Tennessee, with whom he had left his war notebooks, had mailed them back to his parents at the ranch, after Fred himself came home from the war.

Bogey had written one final story during passage on the ship to America, a story about Chrysis, their love affair, and his departure from France. By all available evidence, he never wrote another story after that, and at the ranch, he stored all of his notebooks in the steamer trunk he had brought home with him, and this he locked and put away in the tack room of the barn.

Bogey quickly discovered that all of the girls he had grown up with were long since married with children, or moved away from North Park. And after over a decade in Europe and his years in France, and particularly after having known and loved Chrysis in Paris, the local women of the region seemed uninteresting, nearly incomprehensible to him. It was as if, in addition to having learned to speak French, he had also learned a new language of love that did not translate well in the rural western United States.

Still, Bogey wished to have a family, and in 1932, entirely on a whim, he wrote a letter to the girl Lola, the proprietor's daughter at Mona's brothel in the Port of New York. Lola wrote back and told him that her mother had passed away and that she was now running the establishment. They began corresponding, and finally Lola took a train out west to visit Bogey for two weeks at the ranch. Six months later they were married, and they would have two sons and a daughter.

Except to attend cattle and horse sale rings, and an occasional regional rodeo, in which his sons or daughter were competing, Bogey never left the ranch again. He had framed the childhood drawing Chrysis had given him, and he kept it on the wall of his small office in the ranch house. He put the single photograph he had taken of her into the red Craven "A" cigarette tin, and this he kept tucked away in the back of the drawer of his desk. He was never able to forget that young woman or those extraordinary years in Paris, and despite his long, happy marriage, she remained, to his dying day, the great love of his life.

Bogey's wife, Lola, died of cancer in the spring of 1977. Their three children had long since left the region—their daughter to marry a banker from Grand Island, Nebraska, and their sons to pursue other careers in different parts of the country. Bogey was left alone on the ranch, and in October of 1979, at age 80, as he was moving stray cattle from summer pasture on a U.S. Forest Service grazing lease in the mountains, his horse stepped into a badger hole, fell and rolled over him, crushing his chest. The horse had broken its leg in the hole, and Bogey had just strength enough to pull his grandfather's Colt .45 from the holster, and put the animal out of its misery. Two days later, a Forest Service employee found the old rancher's body still pinned under that of his horse.

The Lambert ranch was purchased from the heirs by a neighboring rancher, and the house and barn were abandoned by the new owner, left to the skunks and rodents, and to rot back to earth. Two decades later, a curious journalist scavenging on the property, came across an old steamer trunk in the tack room of the partially collapsed barn. He jimmied the lock and found inside fourteen handwritten notebooks, full of hundreds of unpublished stories written between 1916-1929, each signed and dated by Bogart Lambert.

Bogey clearly had some premonition of his coming death, for at the end of that final story of 1929, which he had written on the ship back to America, there was a separate note in his handwriting on the last page, dated less than three weeks before the accident that killed him. It reads:

Maybe, if we are lucky, we are allowed to experience one great love in our lifetime. And maybe, if we are very lucky, that love survives, endures until death do us part. More likely, we all pass our days on earth in small bubbles of distinct time, when things are one way for a while, and then before we are even aware of it, they become another way, and another after that. People come and go through our lives, they die, we die, dreams fade finally, or are replaced by other dreams, or just as often by none at all—the absence of dreams. The French have a simple, fatalistic way of expressing the shifting vagaries of life. "C'est comme ça," they say with a shrug, "that's how it is." Here, at the end of my life, I am grateful to take to my grave a beautiful dream that has never died, the memory of love.

Bogart Lambert
Crazy Horse Ranch, North Park, Colorado
September 28, 1979

Acknowledgements

Oddly, I believe that I did more research for this little novel than for any of my others, and throughout the process, I was helped by a great number of people, to all of whom I am deeply indebted, and all of whom deserve to be acknowledged.

My journey began in Boulogne-sur-Mer, France, the birthplace of Gabrielle "Chrysis" Jungbluth, and it was there that the archivist at the mayor's office, Veronique Delpierre, gave me a copy of Chrysis's birth certificate, which set me out on the trail of the young painter's life. In her own time and upon her own initiative, Mademoiselle Delpierre continued to do further invaluable research for me.

Thanks also to Juliette Jestaz, the librarian at La Bibliothèque de l'École Nationale des Beaux-Arts for her cheerful and efficient assistance and advice in further directing me down the path.

Thanks to Professor Claude-Henri Chouard, the historian at the Salon des Indépendants for providing me with archival information about Chrysis Jungbluth's long association with that distinguished institution.

I gratefully thank all of the fine, helpful staff members at La Bibliothèque Nationale de France, where I spent a number of splendid days researching in the winter of 2011. My identity card, granting me access to that magnificent building, remains one of my proudest possessions. I extend similar thanks to the staff of La Bibliothèque de l'Institut National d'Histoire de l'Art, who were all so kind and willing to assist me in my efforts. Of these fine people, I especially thank Emmanuelle Royon, who undertook further research for me, both at her own institution and in Les Archives Nationales.

Special thanks to my friend and *attachée de presse*, Sabine Mille, who helped me immensely in navigating all of the above institutions, which can sometimes seem an intimidating bureaucratic maze for an American with imperfect French language skills.

My faithful French editor, Arnaud Hofmarcher, without whom I would never have been published in that country, put me in touch with the Archives Genealogiques Andriveau. I thank him for that service and for his constant friendship and support. I thank, too, the fine people at Andriveau who provided initial contact information for the family of Chrysis's husband, Roland Narfin, on the island of Martinique. And I thank Franz Narfin, a nephew of Roland's, who directed me to the property where Chrysis and her husband had lived together for many years.

I am especially grateful to my dear friend Dominique Doutrepont, who accompanied me to Martinique in the winter of 2012, and was not only a wonderful traveling companion, but also a great help to me in following Chrysis from France to that beautiful Caribbean island.

In Martinique, Clément Relouzat, another nephew of Chrysis's husband, Roland, who lives on the familial property, received us at his home with tremendous graciousness and hospitality, showed us photographs and documents, the first truly personal items from Chrysis's life I had yet seen; and he took us to her grave. Mr.

Relouzat continued to be a rich source of information and help to me throughout the process of researching this novel, and I owe him a great debt of gratitude. I thank, as well, his charming mother, Solange Relouzat, who, with the same Martiniquais hospitality as her son, invited me to lunch at her home in Paris, and entrusted me with further precious family memories and photographs of Chrysis. Of the same family, I thank Mr. and Mrs. Christie Narfin, who also invited me to their Paris home and showed me early student work of Chrysis.

On the other side of the family, great thanks to Jacqueline Jungbluth, the goddaughter of Chrysis, who gave me access to personal letters of both Chrysis and her father, Colonel Charles Jungbluth.

I thank my costume designer friend, Penny Rose, who provided me with tremendously helpful information regarding Chrysis's wardrobe in the 1920s.

Thanks to my friend, Karine Meyronne, for valuable historical information regarding maritime activities during the Great War, and for insights into a young woman's erotic nature.

My talented painter friend, Amy Metier, was also an important resource in helping me to understand the timeless techniques and motivations of her profession, and those of a young painter of any era, and I thank her.

To my friend and French translator, Sophie Aslanides, I offer my particular and grateful thanks for fully including me in the process of her own stellar work of translation of this manuscript for its original publication in France.

Finally, special love and gratitude to my stepdaughter, Isabella Tudisco-Sadacca, whose mother, Mari Tudisco, first set us out upon the trail of young Chrysis

Jungbluth. Not only did Isabella offer me helpful structural advice regarding this novel, but she also provided invaluable insights into the energies, thought processes, and passions of a young woman artist—territory not always so easy for a male novelist of a certain age to fully enter.

Jim Fergus, Paris, January, 2013

To view the full image of the painting *Orgie*, by Chrysis Jungbluth, Paris, 1928, please visit: www.jimfergus.com

Made in the USA
Columbia, SC
14 February 2018